THE DAUGHTER

50-PLUS CONDO BOOK 2

JANIE OWENS

ONE

ANGIE BARNES LOOKED out the airplane window while the flight landed at Daytona Beach International Airport. She hadn't been in Florida for quite some time and felt more than a little apprehensive about returning home. Will her parents welcome her? Will they greet this visit with great joy or see it as another opportunity for her to mooch? She had a history of sponging off her parents. Oh, yes, she was really good at holding out her hand and asking for more.

She pulled out her phone and dialed. *Better warn them rather than just show up unannounced.*

"Joe!"

"In the bedroom."

"I need you."

Joe Barnes walked into the living room where his wife Rachel was sitting on the couch, the phone in her lap.

"That was Angie," Rachel said without expression or emotion.

Angela was her true name, but no one ever called her

that. She was born near Christmas, and at that time Rachel was fascinated with the idea of Angie the Christmas tree angel. Consequently, her daughter was named Angela, but forever called Angie.

"So? Not good news?" Joe asked as he sat across from her.

"Depends on how you look at it," Rachel said, fixing her eyes on her husband. "She wants to stay with us for a while. She's not sure how long."

"Oh." Joe knew what that meant.

"I'm just not in the frame of mind to fund her living expenses while she searches for her life's purpose or the meaning of life," Rachel said, shaking her head.

"Did you tell her that?"

"Not exactly in those words, but I hinted around."

"If we aren't firm, she will take advantage again," Joe said.

"I haven't forgotten."

"When is she arriving?"

"In a couple hours."

"What?" Joe shot to standing. "Well, we'd better get our stories aligned. We can't let her walk all over us again."

"I totally agree," Rachel said. "But you're the one who caves in." She gave her husband a knowing look.

Joe acknowledged that was true with his grunt. Rachel was much tougher when it came to their only daughter, their only child. And sometimes that fact caused clashes between Angie and her.

"I'll do better," he said, walking toward the hallway. "I'll follow your lead."

"I was really enjoying this last year without the gimme, gimme hand held out," Rachel said, rising.

"Me, too."

They both walked down the hall to the extra bedroom. It would be perfect for Angie while she visited. A door at the entrance to the hall provided privacy from the rest of the unit. A vanity crossed the hall at the end with cabinets and a sink in the center, and a large mirror above. To the left was a door leading to the shower and toilet. To the right, a door to the bedroom.

"I'll have to remove the dog bed, and my clothes from the closet. There isn't much else here," Rachel said, glancing around.

"And the cross on the wall."

"Let it stay. She can just deal with it," Rachel said. "If she's still a Buddhist or whatever she might have become recently, we are a Christian home. She can deal."

"Fine by me."

Angie walked into her parent's condo unit with a backpack over her shoulders, two large suitcases rolling behind her, and a small carrier attached to one of the suitcases. She positioned everything upright after she crossed the threshold and removed the backpack. Angie was fairly tall for having two parents on the short side. Her long legs slinked from under her blue shorts. The matching shirt, tied in front, accentuated her tiny waist. Rachel noticed that her hair was bleached blonde and flowed past her shoulders. It was red the last time they saw her. She didn't have on much makeup, not that she needed it. Angie was a very attractive young woman.

"Hi, guys!" she said, expanding her arms for an embrace.

Of course, Rufus the dog barged in before the parents could hug their daughter. He wiggled between Rachel and Joe and started to lunge at Angie, then stopped just short. Rufus whined and extended one paw toward the woman.

"Aw, so sweet," Angie said, petting the big boy's head. The labradoodle loved the attention and frantically wagged his tail.

"Humph, so well behaved. Is this our dog?" Rachel said. "He always attacks me when I enter."

Rufus and Rachel had history. Rufus always lunged at Rachel when she came in from one of her nights out with the girls. She could write a book about the many incidents she had with him knocking her over, straddling her, and then licking her face with vigor.

"You just have to know how to handle them, Mom," Angie said. "It's all about energy. He recognizes my energy and respects it." Angie continued to stroke Rufus' head.

Rachel was about to respond, but Joe placed his hand in the center of her back to distract her. Then both parents hugged and kissed their daughter, all the while wondering what was this visit going to bring and why was she here?

"Gee, Dad, I see you haven't grown any more hair," Angie cracked with a big smile.

Joe was in his late fifties. He figured his days for having a full head of hair had long passed. He had a clean-shaven face with ordinary features and few wrinkles for a man his age. He was neither fat nor skinny, and in decent physical shape.

"How nice of you to notice," he said.

"Mom, you look great!"

Rachel did look great. She was a cute brunette with a classic bob she had worn with and without bangs for most of her adult life. At fifty-three and holding her figure, Rachel was as pretty as her daughter.

"Thank you. So do you." Rachel maneuvered her daughter toward the living room. "Let's get comfy."

"I've been sitting for hours, or else walking through airports," Angie said. "I'm glad to be on solid ground."

"Where did you fly from?" Joe asked.

"California."

"You've been in California all this time?" Rachel asked.

"Oh, no, I've been in lots of places, but most recently in California," Angie said, sitting back on the off-white couch.

"So, where have you been staying? What does that mean?" Joe asked.

"Well, Dad," Angie said, "I've been in Massachusetts, the United Kingdom, then India, Massachusetts again, and then California. I stayed at ashrams everywhere I traveled."

"Ashrams," Rachel said flatly without facial expression.

"Yes, Mom, ashrams. Perfectly safe to be in. Holy places, you know?"

"I know what an ashram is. I don't know why you were living in them," Rachel said. "And, of course, you haven't communicated with us for at least nine months. Last we heard you were in the States. We didn't know anything about the United Kingdom or India."

"Well, Mom, I didn't think I had to check in with my parents every time I decided to travel," Angie said, a look of exasperation coming over her face. "I *am* twenty-five."

"Your age has nothing to do with this," Joe said. "When you are in a foreign country, we need to know, in case something happens or you disappear."

Angie flung her long hair over her shoulder with a scowl. "Look, nothing happened; nothing was going to happen. I was perfectly safe, end of story."

"Here we go," Rachel said, remembering how obstinate and naïve her daughter could be.

"Angie, you can't live so irresponsibly that you endanger yourself," Joe said.

"I'm not being irresponsible. Gee, Dad!" Angie stood. "I was hoping you guys, after moving to this condo, would relax some. But you're both still so uptight."

Rachel decided to sit back and let Joe handle things.

"Angie, we are your parents. We care about you, always will. If that's being uptight, well, I guess you'd better get used to it," he said. "If you don't like how your parents act, you can live elsewhere."

"No, I can't. I don't have anywhere else to go right now. You're stuck with me for a while." Angie threw a cutesy smile at her father. "Besides, I know you've missed me."

Rachel wasn't so sure that last part was true. She didn't miss the chaos Angie tended to create in their lives. She wanted a calm, peaceful life. All the unique people who lived in this fifty plus condominium that she managed were enough entertainment and chaos for her. At least they didn't live under her roof.

"Okay, what do you say we get your bags in your room?" Rachel said.

"I'll carry the bags," Joe said, rising.

"Dad, suitcases have wheels now," Angie said. "They roll."

"Whatever," Joe answered with a wave of his hand.

As the three approached, a loud protest erupted from the area where the suitcases had been dropped.

"What was that noise?" Rachel asked.

"Oh, that's just Precious," Angie said.

"Precious what?" Joe asked.

"Precious, my cat," Angie said.

"You have a cat?" Rachel asked.

"Yes. Is that unusual?" Angie said. "I've always had cats, ever since childhood. You know that. Cats are my passion."

"You never mentioned a cat," Joe said. "We didn't know about a cat."

"So, what's the big deal? You have pets," Angie said, stroking Rufus' head as he stood beside her.

"There is a limit on the number of animals we can have in one unit, Angie," Rachel said. "I manage this condo. I can't have any more animals than I currently have. One dog, one cat. Period."

"Well, I won't be here long, maybe, so it shouldn't be a

problem," Angie said. "I'll be gone before it becomes an issue."

Rachel had doubts about that.

"There is also a limit on how long you can visit, since you're not fifty years old," Joe said.

"Gee, so many rules! How do you stand it?" Angie said.

Joe looked at his wife and decided not to respond.

"Okay, let's get your luggage into your room," Rachel said.

All three paraded down the hallway toward the second bedroom. Joe pulled the suitcases behind him and then swung them onto the queen bed. Angie handled the backpack and carrier with Precious inside.

"Oh, this is nice," Angie said when she entered the bedroom. "I like the soft aqua walls."

"And your bathroom is over there, just past the counter and sink," Rachel said, pointing across the hallway.

"Nice. Private," Angie said.

"Yes, it is. And I expect you to keep everything nice while you're here," Rachel said.

"Oh, Mom, I'm not five!"

Rachel didn't comment. Sometimes it seemed like her daughter acted like a five-year-old.

"And the litter box is where?" Angie asked.

"Very conveniently in your bathroom." Rachel said. "Introduce your cat to it. I'll have to place another one in the other bathroom for Benny now. I suggest closing the door at the end of the hallway until we can acquaint all the animals."

"Good idea, Mom. I'll let Precious out after you leave."

"Okay, then. We'll let you unpack and rest if you want," Rachel said, turning to leave.

"Thanks, guys," Angie said. She sounded sincere.

"Later," Joe said.

TWO

AFTER ANGIE HAD UNPACKED and rested briefly, the first attempt was made to introduce Precious to the rest of the animals living in the condo. They began by placing Precious, in her carrier, in the center of the living room. The cat began softly growling inside the carrier as Rufus approached. No one had seen Bennie since Angie arrived. So typical of a cat, Bennie was no doubt hiding.

"Rufus, this is Precious," Rachel said, holding onto Rufus' collar as she placed him in front of the carrier.

Precious let out a hideous wail and began spitting at Rufus from behind the bars of the carrier. Rufus backed away, as if he wasn't sure what was inside. Perhaps he had never experienced such an out-roar from another animal? Rachel was alarmed over the cat's reaction. Rufus, while very large in size, was a true wimp. He wouldn't hurt anything walking or crawling.

"Oh, my," Rachel said.

"Don't worry. Precious is a doll," Angie said.

Rufus wasn't so sure. Rachel wasn't so sure, either. Joe just stood watching the scene play out. Then the dog cowered, looking at the carrier and the vixen within from a distance of four feet.

"I should let her out to meet Rufus," Angie said.

"Are you sure?" Rachel asked. "She doesn't appear to like the idea of meeting new friends."

"Oh, no problem," Angie said, unlatching the carrier. Angie swung the cage door open and a fluffy white Persian cat pranced out, full of attitude.

Precious surveyed her surroundings briefly, then promptly planted her abundant behind on the floor. She made a little purp sound that made Rachel feel that all was going well. Until it wasn't.

Rufus, who was still four feet away from the carrier, stood and let out one loud woof, to which Precious took exception, letting out her own vocal response to convey her displeasure. She hissed and spit in the direction of the big dog, who immediately cowered to the floor again. Precious began growling at Rufus, edging towards him in a slinky and menacing manner.

"Whoa, wait!" Rachel cried, waving her hands.

"Hey, leave Rufus alone, cat!" Joe said, moving towards the two animals. He positioned himself between the cat and dog, hoping to thwart any aggression.

"You guys, gee, it's okay," Angie said. "She's harmless."

Angie reached down, picked up Precious and turned away from Rufus with the cat in her arms.

"I'll take her into my bedroom until Rufus gets adjusted."

Angie carried Precious into her bedroom and closed the door behind her. Shortly thereafter, she returned to be with her parents.

"It's all good; no biggy," Angie said.

While Angie didn't recognize any problem, her parents had another view. Joe and Rachel exchanged looks, not at all sure everything was okay.

"So, when do we eat?" Angie asked.

"Right now," Rachel said, turning to other matters. "Get to the table, everything is ready."

Everyone sat down at the table, which had already been set for dinner, and Rachel brought out the meal. Joe led the grace.

"What are your plans while you're here," Joe asked as he passed the large salad bowl over to Angie.

"I'm not totally sure. I need time to think, to meditate on my future," she answered, heaping salad into her bowl. "Being so near the beach, the peace it brings, I should receive my answers." Angie passed the large bowl to her mother.

Rachel stifled a comment, silently accepting the bowl. This was so typical of Angie. Nothing had changed. She was still in Lala Land, her head in the clouds, no sense of direction.

"How long do you think it will take to receive those answers?" Rachel finally asked.

"There's no such thing as time in the universe. It takes as long as it takes," Angie said.

Rachel heard Joe give a short sigh from across the table.

"Well, I'm predicting the universe will answer your needs quickly, realizing your parents aren't going to bankroll your meditations for very long," he said, stuffing his mouth with a forkful of salad.

"Oh, Daddy, you're so silly," Angie said, giggling. She always used the endearing term of daddy when she wanted something or was trying to smooth over an issue. "I might even go back to school."

"And study what?" Rachel asked. "You've been a perpetual student for years. To my knowledge, you haven't held a real job."

"Life isn't all about making money, Mom." Angie rolled her eyes, her mother's habit.

Joe shot his wife a quick look and she resisted the urge to speak, swallowing her words with lettuce.

"What your mother means is, at some point in life everyone has to support themselves. We can't support you," Joe said. "We won't pay for more school, rent on an apartment, your clothes, nothing more. *You* have to start paying your own expenses."

A slight frown formed between Angie's eyes.

"But, Daddy…"

"No buts, Angie." Rachel found her voice. "Get a job, save your money, and move out. It's time for the birdie to fly."

Angie put her fork down, looking from one parent to the next to see which was weakest. Both held firm expressions as they chewed their salad. So, she focused on her father, the usual weak link.

"Daddy, finding a job could take some time. As Mom said, I haven't had a real job, so it could be difficult landing one," Angie said, intently staring at her father.

"True. But as long as you are relentlessly seeking a job, we will understand. Yes, it might take a little time to land a good one," Joe agreed. "So, in the meantime, you get a job at McDonalds or Wal-Mart to sustain you."

Angie's eyes flew open in surprise. Her father had never talked to her in such a manner.

"But, Daddy! Flipping burgers? You can't be serious."

Joe looked at his daughter evenly and spoke calmly. "There are people who would love to have a job flipping burgers. And you know why? Because they need the money to survive," Joe said, looking back at his salad bowl. "Just like you."

The room grew very quiet. The only noise was the sound of crunching salad.

THREE

RACHEL PLOPPED down in the chair behind her desk, delighted to be in her office. It wasn't a large office, but had enough size to accommodate several file cabinets, her desk and chair, and the guest chair positioned in front. Behind her was the mini fridge where she kept water bottles. All but one wall was glass, which gave her the advantage of seeing who was approaching, whether from the outside or within the building. She happily put on her condo manager cap and cast off her mother's hat. Whatever the day brought; she was eager to greet every event.

LuAnn Riley was the first one to come through the door. Her blonde hair fell past her shoulders, just like one would expect of a country singer. LuAnn could have passed for Dolly Parton's sister, since she had a similar face with a figure to match. And long nails.

"Hi, honey."

"Have a seat," Rachel said, pointing at the chair across from the desk. "What's up?"

"I was just wanting to know if you and Joe would like to

come hear me sing this weekend and meet Derks?" Her pretty face shone with joy.

Derks Ford was LuAnn's boyfriend. They were rather new as a couple, but the situation looked promising, according to LuAnn.

"I think we can do that," Rachel said. "Do you mind if we bring Angie?"

"Who's Angie?"

"Our daughter. She's visiting."

"Oh, honey, that would be wonderful," she drawled. "Y'all come and bring Angie along. She'll have a good time."

"Yes, I think she would enjoy herself."

"How long is she visiting for?"

"That's a very good question," Rachel said with a sigh. "I have no idea."

"Oh, one of those situations." LuAnn nodded her head like she understood. Although she had been married three times, LuAnn did not have any children.

"Yes, but Joe is really on board this time. I don't think he'll cave to her whims."

"Nothing like a daughter batting her eyelashes at her daddy. Works every time," LuAnn said. "Did for me."

"Are you meeting us later at the clubhouse?" Rachel asked.

"I'll be there at five. Have some errands to run and then get my nails done." LuAnn held out one hand and wiggled her fingers.

"See ya then."

No sooner had the door closed than Ruby Moskowitz walked into the office. Ruby was the building's most flamboyant resident. Her preferred clothing was a bathing suit that revealed everything that no one wanted to see. At the age of ninety-something, the only things she had to expose were skinny limbs adorned by knobby joints with creped skin as a covering. With flaming red hair piled on top of her head and red lipstick, she was quite a sight to behold as she strutted around the pool, doing her best model walk.

"Hi, Ruby," Rachel said. She was quite fond of the old woman, despite the heavy gardenia scent that followed her everywhere. While most of the female residents thought she was brazen, mainly due to their jealousy, Rachel knew of her compassionate side.

"Hi. I just wanted you to know that Loretta is under the weather." The way Ruby made her statement, it sounded to Rachel like she was more than a little concerned.

"What's wrong with her?"

"Well, I'm not sure," she answered, sitting in the chair in front of the desk. "She's coughing a lot. I told her to go to the doctor, but she doesn't want to. She hates doctors; says she'll take cough medicine instead."

"A woman her age shouldn't mess around with a cough."

"I know. I told her that."

"Do you want me to talk to her?"

"Not yet. If I can't get through to her, I'll let you know."

The door to the office opened and Joe stuck his head in. "Just so you know, the new tenant is moving in on the eighth floor."

"Okay, thanks, Joe," replied Rachel, turning back to Ruby.

"So, I'm going to pick up some chicken noodle soup for Loretta," Ruby said, standing. "Can't hurt, might help."

"Good idea, Ruby. Keep me informed, okay?"

"I will."

After Ruby left, Rachel sat back in thought. Loretta was an elegant woman in her middle eighties. She was a good Christian woman with a past that no one would have ever guessed by current appearances. Loretta had been a high-profile detective in Nevada. Ruby was Loretta's Confidential Informant, bringing important information about the influential elite that she associated with due to her prominence as a fashion model.

The women had not seen each other in decades. Ruby deliberately moved away because she feared repercussions from some of the prison releases who might come looking for Loretta. Then when Loretta coincidentally moved into the same condo, Ruby again was afraid of being discovered and continued to avoid Loretta. It wasn't until recently that they had become very close friends, even taking a Hawaiian cruise together. Rachel had great respect for Loretta's wisdom and had asked her counsel in the past.

"Enough," she said aloud. She had work to do.

Rachel rode the elevator to the eighth floor where the new tenant was moving into a condo unit. And it wasn't just any condo unit. It was the one where her friend Eneida had lived, until she was murdered. In that unit. It took weeks before it was cleared by the police for entry. The condominium owners eventually foreclosed on it and had to pay for renovations. After repairs were done on the wall where a portion had been removed as evidence and then painted, the carpeting was removed, and tile was installed in its place. Rachel had wondered if it would ever be rented out or purchased?

Rachel exited the elevator and turned onto the walkway that stretched outside across each of the twelve floors of the condominium. It was an open walkway with an iron fence to prevent anyone from falling below. Immediately, she saw the movement of people walking into the previously vacant unit. Several men were hoisting furniture and boxes. It appeared that a professional crew had been hired to accomplish this move for the new resident.

Rachel came to the door where all the action was taking place. A young man poked his head out when Rachel approached. He was dark haired, clean shaven, and quite handsome. He wore a black tee-shirt, black jeans, and was slender in body.

"Hi, I'm Rachel Barnes, the condo manger," she said, extending her hand toward him.

"Yeah, great, I'm Josh," he said in response, extending his hand as well. "Josh Brigham. Just moving in now." Josh smiled down at her. He was tall, much taller than Rachel.

"Is everything going well?" Rachel asked.

"Oh, yeah, what could be wrong?" Josh smiled broadly at Rachel.

"I hope nothing," she said. "If you do have any problems, let me know. My office is on the first floor."

"I don't anticipate any problems," he answered. "Thank you for caring."

"Not a problem, Josh," she said, turning to leave.

Rachel's immediate impression was that of a very polite young man. Being young, though, she hoped his youthful behaviors wouldn't become an issue. She couldn't help wondering why he was moving into an over fifty condo. Perhaps he was the son of the new resident, maybe helping him to move in? She didn't know, so she decided to speak with the president of the condo board and the applicant himself. When she returned to her office, she dug out the application for residency and called the applicant, John Brigham.

"Yes," a male voice said.

"Hi, I am Rachel Barnes, the manager of the Breezeway Condominiums that you are moving into."

"Okay, yes." He paused, waiting for her response.

"Well, I met a young man today who I imagine is your son? His name was Josh."

Rachel didn't hear any response to her question, so she continued. "Anyway, he was very polite and, I guess, supervising the move," she said. "I haven't met you, personally, Mr. Brigham, I only have paperwork here on my desk that shows you purchased a unit. I presume he is your son? I mean, people under fifty aren't allowed to purchase a condo unit here."

There was a brief silence before the man spoke.

"That is my condo. But there is no need to concern yourself, young lady."

"What?"

"I will be in town in a few days. Josh is handling everything, so don't worry," the man answered.

"I was merely asking…"

"As I said, I will be in town soon. Josh will handle everything in my absence, so there is no reason for your concern," he said. "I look forward to meeting you."

And with that, the man hung up the phone.

Rachel sat back in her chair, not sure what to make of the conversation. She wished the condo president would be more forthcoming in these matters. How was she to know what was happening with the sales of the units if she wasn't informed? This was a unique situation where the condo association had foreclosed on the unit and resold it. She had not been informed about the new owners, except to know the names and the approximate date of arrival.

The next call Rachel made was to the condo board president, Charles Amos.

"Hello, Rachel. What can I do for you today?" Charles sounded cheery.

"My call is regarding the Brighams. The son is moving everything in today. His name is Josh," she said. "I also spoke with the father, John Brigham, on the phone. I wasn't clear about the arrangements, given we are an over fifty condominium. Josh is obviously much younger than fifty. His name isn't on the forms as owner, either."

"Nothing to worry about, Rachel," he said. "Everything has been worked out."

"What does that mean?"

"It means, don't worry about it," Charles said.

What was happening? Two men in a short period of time were telling her not to worry about the details of this unit. What was so special about the Brighams?

"I don't understand the secrecy surrounding this unit."

"There isn't any secrecy, Rachel. Mr. Brigham will be in town soon. Josh is moving his father into the unit," he said. "End of story."

"Well, okay," she said. But she didn't believe that was the end of the story. There was something fishy about this.

Rachel thought it especially odd that someone would purchase a unit where a murder had been committed, especially when other units were available. By law, full disclosure was required to any potential buyer. Who wants a unit where a murder, a gruesome murder, no less, had taken place? Unless they were a mortician or Stephen King.

FOUR

PENELOPE HARDWOOD WALKED into Rachel's office. She turned to speak to someone still in the hallway. "Just wait for me," she said, then turned toward Rachel.

"Good morning, Penelope."

Penelope was a sweet woman and a long-time resident in the Breezeway Condominium. She was also Rachel's spy. Whenever someone was misbehaving, Penelope had an uncanny way of being present and then reporting the incident to Rachel.

"Yes, it is a good morning, isn't it?" Penelope answered. "I have my condo fee here."

The old woman placed a check on Rachel's desk, sliding it toward her with one bony finger.No one had ever seen her wearing anything but a loose housedress with a heavy cardigan hugged close to her body. Even in the common ninety-five-degree temperatures of Florida. Today was no exception.

"Thank you," Rachel said. "Who's in the hallway?"

"Oh, that's just Alfred. He doesn't have his check ready yet."

Alfred Thorn was an elderly man who frequently wore lightweight jackets, giving him a formal appearance for Florida. He had very white hair that he chose to wear grown near his collar, and very bushy white eyebrows that Rachel longed to trim. Alfred and Penelope had apparently become friends, much to Rachel's surprise. Penelope was very proper, so Rachel surmised that Alfred's formal appearance had been an appealing factor.

"He can come in," Rachel suggested.

"No, he can just wait for me," she said. "I'm done here anyway."

"Okay, well, have a nice day, Penelope."

"I will. You, too, dear," she said, clasping her blue sweater close and walking into the hallway where Alfred was patiently waiting. Evidently, having an afterthought, Penelope returned.

"You should probably know, that widow is making a spectacle of herself."

"What widow?" Rachel asked.

"The one on the sixth floor, Ethel Borenstein. The one with the curly blue hair."

"Oh, that widow. What's she doing?"

"For starters, she's hanging out with Ruby at the pool."

"What's wrong with that?"

"Well, she's not properly dressed. She wears two-piece bathing suits, usually purple ones."

Ethel was not even five foot tall and was as round as she was tall. Her penchant for wearing revealing bathing suits began after her husband died and she started being friends with Ruby. Rachel understood Penelope's opinion of the old lady's attire. She looked like a mini Sumo wrestler with wiggly flesh hanging out everywhere.

"Penelope, we don't have any rules concerning residents' attire. If Ethel wants to wear purple two-piece bathing suits, she can do that." Maybe the color accentuated her blue hair?

The old lady stretched her cardigan covered body in a superior manner, looking sideways at Rachel. "Well, *I* wouldn't be caught dead in what she wears. It's just unseemly."

Rachel silently agreed but did not share her opinion. She knew Penelope wouldn't be caught dead wearing any sort of revealing clothing, let alone a two-piece bathing suit.

"Maybe I can suggest to her wearing a coverup when out in public," Rachel offered.

"At the very least," Penelope said, then turned to leave.

Ethel had lived at the condo for many years with her husband. After he passed, she seemed to act like a woman set free. She appeared to be living as she pleased, going out with other women, making new friends, such as Ruby, and hanging out at the pool in scanty bathing suits. Rachel wasn't about to tell her how to dress. That was the old woman's prerogative. But maybe she could suggest a coverup.

"Don't you have any wine in the house?" Angie asked as she rummaged around in the refrigerator. "I don't see any in here."

"No, we don't keep alcohol in the house," Rachel said, looking over her shoulder from the kitchen counter.

"Wine isn't alcohol. It's not liquor, it's wine. Just wine," Angie said with authority.

"Actually, Angie," Rachel said, turning from the counter where she was preparing a salad for dinner, "wine and beer have alcohol content. Maybe not as high a percentage as in liquor, but it is present. You can get just as drunk on wine as vodka, for instance."

"Really? Hmm. Since when did you become such an

expert on the matter?" Angie asked, sitting at the little table in the kitchen.

"Since I discovered I am a diabetic. I had to learn all sorts of things about eating properly for my condition." This was the first time she had mentioned her illness to Angie.

Angie's expression changed after hearing her mother is a diabetic.

"You? A diabetic?" Angie said in amazement.

"Yes. Unfortunately. I almost drowned in the bathtub due to diabetes. Your father found me just in time and I went to the emergency room. That's when I was diagnosed, but I had my suspicions." Rachel turned back to the task at the counter. "If you had called home once in a while, I would have told you."

"Sorry. Wow. A diabetic. So, you don't keep alcohol of any kind in the house for that reason?" Angie asked.

"Correct. Your father doesn't drink, I don't drink, so, why have any in the house?" Rachel said.

"I understand that. Okay, no big deal. I rarely drink anyway," Angie said, rising. "I'm going to feed Precious."

Angie opened the door to the hallway and found Precious standing right at the opening. Seeing this as her opportunity for escape, Precious leaped forward into freedom. She streaked through the dining area and then straight into Joe and Rachel's bedroom where she disappeared under the bed. It didn't take long for a commotion to erupt because also under the bed was Benny.

Angie and Rachel ran toward the noise coming from under the bed where both cats were delivering hisses and growls. This was Benny's first encounter with Precious. Under the bed was his territory, and he made clear his distaste over the invasion, his growls growing louder with accompanying snarls. All the commotion brought Rufus into the bedroom to investigate. He began barking toward the ruckus.

"Precious, get out of there," Angie said, lifting the bed skirt as she peaked underneath the bed. "Come here."

"Benny, be nice," Rachel said in a stern voice. "Meet your new friend."

"New friend? Are you kidding? They're going to tear each other apart!" Angie shrieked.

"I'll get a broom to chase them out," Rachel said, leaving the room.

The fight intensified by the time Rachel returned to the war zone. Given the thumping sound on the wooden floor, she figured they had made physical contact with each other and were rolling around underneath the bed. At least it sounded like that was happening. Meanwhile, Rufus continued his serenade. Rachel stuck the broom under the bed as Angie held the bed skirt up so her mother could see underneath. She made contact with the rolling balls of fur and pressed them out from under the bed. Both cats appeared, spitting and hissing, then ran from the room in different directions. Rufus gave chase, not knowing which cat to go after. He quickly gave up and laid by the sliders leading to the balcony.

Angie gasped, "Look at the white fur! My poor cat! Oh, my Precious."

"Calm down. She ran out, so she's not hurt," Rachel said. "She just lost a little fur. No big deal."

"No big deal?" Apparently, it was a big deal to Angie. "She's a purebred. She has papers!"

"Well, she uses the litter box, just like Benny," Rachel said. "Precious is a cat. Get over it."

Angie looked at her mother with an indignant expression. "She's my baby."

"Well, keep your baby in your room so she doesn't get her feathers ruffled again."

"Precious, sweetie. Mommy is coming," Angie called as she walked toward her bedroom, closing the door.

As soon as that door closed, the front door opened. In walked Joe.

"Hey,"

"Hey yourself," Rachel said as she walked to the kitchen. "You just missed the big fight."

"You and Angie get into it?"

"No. Precious and Benny."

"Oh. Who won?"

"Hard to tell, although Precious lost some fur," Rachel said, reaching into the refrigerator for salad dressing. "Precious and Angie are in the bedroom now."

"How'd the fight come about?"

"Precious escaped and ran under our bed. Benny was there, naturally, so, the fight ensued," she said.

"Hey, that's where Benny sleeps most of the time."

"I know."

Angie came out of her bedroom with a concerned look on her face.

"Daddy, Precious was in a fight."

"So I heard," Joe said. Rachel knew he was about to be manipulated.

"You have to do something about Benny," Angie said, sitting down at the dining room table.

"Like what? He lives here." Joe joined his daughter at the table.

"But Precious is here now," Angie said.

"Precious is a guest. Precious will be leaving when you leave," Joe said. "Maybe you need to move a little faster to make that happen."

"But Daddy!"

"Okay, you two, go wash hands, dinner is done," Rachel interrupted. She placed the salad bowl on the table.

Joe went to the kitchen to wash his hands, Angie to their sink in the couple's bathroom.

"So, how is the job hunt going?" Joe asked as he sat at the table again.

Angie's head popped up quickly after she sat. "What job hunt? I'm concerned about my cat."

"The job hunt we discussed when you first arrived." Joe helped himself to some salad and passed the bowl to his wife. "You are supposed to be looking for employment."

Angie sighed when she accepted the bowl from her mother. "Well, I haven't done that. I only arrived yesterday. So, I've been at the beach, meditating."

"I can see that. You look a little pink in the face," Joe said, reaching for the dressing. "Tomorrow I want you pounding the streets for a job. Any job."

"Any job?" Angie asked.

"Any respectable job. Even if it's minimum wage," Joe said. "Let's have grace before we eat."

The discussion stopped long enough for Joe to say grace.

"Like, where?" Angie asked.

"Try the mall," Rachel suggested. "There are lots of restaurants in that area, too. A plethora of opportunities for jobs."

Angie looked across the table at her mother. "Really? You want me to work in the mall?"

"I did when I was your age. Actually, I was younger," Rachel said, churning her salad around in the bowl with her fork.

Angie looked over at her father. "Daddy?"

"That's a good idea. So are the restaurants. Lots of jobs out that way," he said, smiling at his daughter. "Lots of opportunities for you, sweetheart."

Angie stuffed her mouth full of salad, silently chewing rather than arguing with her parents. Rachel knew what her daughter was thinking: *A job? Working at the mall?* The prospect of working did not appeal to Angie. She had never held a real job, and Rachel suspected she didn't want to now. The necessity escaped her thinking. She imagined that Angie was quite content to allow her parents to pay for everything. Well, that was not happening. Not this time.

FIVE

TWO DAYS LATER, Angie entered the elevator on the ground floor. Before the door closed, a hand reached between the doors, pushing them aside. In walked a handsome man. He was clean shaven and had black hair cut short over his ears with a long bang sweeping across his forehead.

"What floor?" she asked, looking him squarely in the face.

"Eight," he said, returning her look.

Angie immediately wished she had worn something more revealing. But she had been job seeking, so she had on a conservative pair of black slacks and a simple white shirt. Her hair was pulled into a high topknot that showed off the gold hoops hanging from her ears.

"I'm on four," Angie said, pushing both floors.

"So, we're distant neighbors; four floors apart," he said. "I'm Josh Brigham."

"Angie Barnes," she said, reaching her hand out towards his.

"Barnes?" he said, taking her hand in his. "A relation to the manager?"

Josh was dressed in black, except for his sandals. He had

strong legs extending from his black shorts and his arms and chest sported cut muscles under his tee-shirt.

"She's my mother."

"Nice."

The elevator binged to signal it had arrived at the next floor.

"This is me," Angie said, stepping out and turning quickly back. "See ya around."

Josh raised his hand in response.

Angie walked into her parents' condo.

"I'm in here," Rachel said from the kitchen.

"Hi," Angie said. "I just met a really good-looking guy on the elevator."

Rachel ran through her mind all the men she could imagine Angie thinking good looking. There was only one meeting that description.

"You met Josh?"

"Yes. And he's a hunk."

Rachel understood how Angie could say that. Josh was a hunk, in her opinion as well.

"Precious needs your attention," Rachel said, untying the white apron around her waist. She was trying to keep her white pants and top presentable until Joe arrived home. "She's been clawing at the door to get out."

"Okay," Angie said, turning toward the door separating the dining room from the hallway. "My Precious misses me."

Angie reached down as she opened the door to prevent Precious from escaping again. Pushing the cat back with her hand, she squeezed between the door and the jamb, successfully preventing Precious from having another rendezvous with Benny.

Rachel went to the balcony to enjoy the late afternoon

sun. She put her sandaled feet on the footrest and leaned her head back against the plush chair, taking in a relaxing breath of sea air. From this position, she could see the residents enjoying the pool below. Beside the pool was a lovely garden, filled with a variety of flowering bushes and plants. Beyond the garden was the sand and Atlantic Ocean. A beautiful, restful view.

Nothing appeared unusual to her, except Alfred was trailing behind Penelope as she walked around the pool. Penelope never actually got into the pool, preferring to walk around it a couple times each day. Rachel suspected this was her form of exercise. On this day, Penelope wore a heavy pink cardigan as she cautiously stepped around the pool. Alfred was the unusual part, not the sweater.

Ruby was also present, sunning herself by the pool in a hot pink bathing suit. The woman's skin was so tanned from years of sunbathing that it hung from her bony frame, draping down like brown crepe paper. She wore a sunhat to keep her collection of wrinkles from multiplying on her face. Such a character.

Rachel heard the front door close behind her.

"Joe?" she called out.

"Yes, it's me," he said, placing a bag from a store on the dining room table.

Joe walked across the floor to the balcony where Rachel sat, plopping himself down beside her. He looked over at his wife and said, "Hi."

"Hi, you," Rachel said.

"Where's Angie?" Joe asked.

"Right here, Dad," Angie said as she approached the balcony.

"Join us," Rachel said, motioning toward the other chair.

Angie sat, putting her bare feet on the footstool beside her mother's feet.

"Did you go job hunting today?" Joe asked.

"Yes, I did," Angie said. "All day. Just like yesterday."

"So, what happened?" Rachel asked.

"Well, this isn't the time of year to find a retail job, so I've discovered," Angie said. "Nothing at the mall is hiring, and the few shops I ventured to outside the mall aren't hiring, either. The end of the Christmas season is not the time to seek employment. So, retail is out, I'm afraid."

"Sorry, kid," Joe said.

"It's okay. I got a job anyway."

"What!" both parents said as they sat straight up in their chairs.

"Where?" Joe asked first.

"At a little burger joint on the beachside. Family owned," Angie said. "Brian's Burgers."

"That's not far from here," Rachel said.

"No, it's not and that is an advantage. I can walk to work." Angie let her head fall back onto the chair. "I won't have to borrow your car."

"Well, Angie, that is great news," Joe said. "I'm proud of you."

"Thanks, Dad."

"And I'm proud of you, too," Rachel said.

Angie smiled to herself, obviously pleased that her parents were proud of her.

Rachel knocked on Loretta's door and waited. She did not anticipate the eighty-six-year old would come bounding to the door. When Loretta finally open it, Rachel was taken aback. Normally perfectly coiffed and immaculately dressed, the woman standing before her resembled none of that.

"Good morning, Loretta," Rachel said. "May I come in?"

"Of course, dear," she said, standing back to allow Rachel to enter. "Let's sit at the table."

Rachel walked over to the lovely mahogany table in the dining room, taking a seat in the first chair. A beautiful silver tea set was centered on the table. Rachel could see other silver pieces inside the china cabinet against the wall. Farther away was the living area, which was appointed with elegant French Provincial furniture. The fabric looked to be white silk. Paintings adorned the walls that were originals. The woman had good taste.

Loretta walked over slowly and sat down at the head of the table. The smell of Vicks VapoRub filled Rachel's nostrils.

"Loretta, Ruby is very concerned about your health," Rachel said. "She came into the office again today to tell me you still hadn't rallied or gone to the doctor."

Loretta let out a deep sigh, looking weary, and then she started to cough. Her coloring was pale, her lips forming a thin line across her face before she spoke. "She means well."

"I know she does," Rachel agreed. "But you don't look good, Loretta. Don't you think it's time to see a doctor and find out what's wrong?"

Loretta gathered her purple robe close and looked down at the purple pompoms attached to her slippers. The front of her white hair was loosely tucked behind her ears and the rest was pulled back into a sloppy ponytail, a style Rachel had never seen her wear.

"Ruby has been badgering me to go," she said, looking up at Rachel's face. "I guess I should. But I hate doctors."

"How long have you been feeling sick and coughing?"

"About two weeks."

"Loretta, that is much too long a time not to see a doctor. I will take you myself if you like," Rachel said gently.

"No, dear, you have too much to do," Loretta said, leaning back into the chair. "I'll have Ruby take me."

"Does she still drive?"

"Yes, but rather poorly," Loretta said, allowing a slight grin. "But she's capable of getting me there."

"Okay, then. That makes me feel better," Rachel said, standing and then smoothing the creases in her turquoise pants with her hands. "I want you to call me and tell me what the doctor says."

"I will. Promise," Loretta said, shakily rising from the chair.

"I'll let myself out, don't you bother, okay?" Rachel said, extending her hand toward the old lady, touching her arm.

"Yes, dear. Thank you for coming." And with that, Loretta turned her back and walked toward her bedroom, obviously weak. "I will make an appointment," she said over her shoulder.

SIX

RACHEL WAS ALMOST ready to close the office when Ruby entered. She looked a bit breathless and a touch frantic.

"Ruby, what's happening?" Rachel asked.

"Loretta has pneumonia," Ruby said, collapsing into the chair. "She's in the hospital. I just knew it. I knew something bad was wrong."

"Oh, Ruby, I am so sorry," Rachel said, stepping from behind her desk. "What can I do to help?" Rachel placed a hand on Ruby's shoulder.

"I don't guess anything," Ruby said, shaking her head. "I just can't lose Loretta, just can't."

That statement broke Rachel's heart. To have been such close friends, and then estranged for so many years, and now to come back together again, and then this happens.

"Ruby, it's going to be all right. Really, it will."

Ruby looked up at Rachel, wearing an expression that clearly showed she had doubts, and then her eyes began to fill with tears. Rachel bent and grabbed Ruby in her arms and hugged her. "Ruby, Ruby, it will all be good. You'll see."

Rachel allowed the old woman to cry quietly into her

shoulder. After a short time, Ruby sat straighter and Rachel pulled her arms back and stood upright.

"Better now?" Rachel asked. She loved both these women. Even though they were elderly, she felt like they were her friends. She cared what happened to them.

Ruby nodded her head. "Better."

She rose from the chair and headed toward the door, turning around before she left.

"Thanks, Rachel."

"Keep me posted about Loretta," Rachel said.

"I will."

Joe pulled a chair out for Rachel at the round table nearest the stage. Angie seated herself beside her mother, and Joe sat next to his wife. LuAnn was on stage singing at a new place, the Brass Rail. It was located on the beachside, same as the place she had previously played. It didn't take long for a server to arrive to take their order. Everyone ordered a soda.

"She's pretty," Angie said, tucking a strand of hair behind her ear. "I like her outfit."

LuAnn was wearing thigh-high black boots with a long rose-colored skirt flowing over. A slit in the skirt crept up her leg well above the knee. The top she wore was a shiny white fabric with long sleeves and a plunging neckline. LuAnn's hands playfully touched her blonde hair that was pulled into a tousled updo. Rachel noticed that her exceptionally long nails were the exact shade of rose as the skirt. She thought LuAnn looked drop dead gorgeous.

Once she completed singing the song, LuAnn reached behind for her guitar. Rachel chuckled because the guitar was snow white with rose-colored lip prints. This was one of LuAnn's twenty-five guitar collection that she used to accent her outfits. When LuAnn began singing again, one of the guitarists in the band stepped forward to accompany her. He was a good-looking man, with blond hair and a matching goatee. Standing a little taller than LuAnn, he was slender in his blue jeans and plaid shirt. They were a handsome couple, both being blond and good-looking.

"Is that Derks?" Joe asked, leaning toward Rachel.

"I guess so," Rachel said. "LuAnn said he plays in this band."

"They sound great," Angie said, now all smiles and clapping her hands.

Angie was correct. The couple's voices harmonized well. Consequently, they were attracting increasing audiences each week since they began playing there. The band and LuAnn expected to have their booking extended.

Once the set ended, LuAnn came off the stage, pushing the blond-haired man over to their table.

"Hi, y'all. This is Derks, everybody," LuAnn said, her lovely face beaming at them as she held onto Derks' arm.

"LuAnn, this is my daughter Angie. You know Joe," Rachel said. "Nice to meet you, Derks." Rachel shook his hand.

Joe stood to shake hands and greet Derks. He gave LuAnn a quick peck on the cheek. Angie remained seated, smiling at everyone. LuAnn took the remaining chair with Derks standing behind her.

"You guys are so great together," Rachel said. "And LuAnn, I love your outfit. Those boots are crazy."

"Oh, thank you, honey," LuAnn said. "It's just something from my closet."

"I'd like to see that closet. I look like plain Jane over here," Angie said, glancing down at herself. All she had worn were simple blue jeans, sneakers, and a red shirt.

"Well, you'll have to come over sometime and take a peek at my outfits," LuAnn warmly said. "And my guitar collection." She reached to place her hand on the young woman's arm.

"The one up there is quite spectacular," Angie said, pointing toward the stage.

LuAnn laughed. "I got this crazy idea to kiss the guitar all over. I liked how it looked, so I put a sealer over the lip prints. Voila, there she is!"

Rachel watched Derks carefully as he spoke or reacted to LuAnn. He appeared to be genuinely caring and respectful. She liked the crinkles that formed around his eyes when he smiled at her. Maybe this relationship would be a keeper.

Before long, Derks and LuAnn returned to the stage to perform their next set. Rachel and family stayed through the set and then left for home.

Since Angie didn't have to report for work until two o'clock, she decided to indulge in a little sun that morning. Wearing a cute, blue-and-white polka-dot bikini, she stretched out her lean body on the lounge chair after applying protection from the burning rays, gathering her long hair over to one side, and letting it fall over the edge. Just as she was closing her eyes, she heard a splash as someone entered the water. Opening her eyes, she saw the hunk climbing out of the pool. His body glistened, the water droplets clinging to his skin as he returned to the diving board. Angie watched the muscles in his back and legs with interest as he walked and then climbed the steps to the diving board. He was wearing very small, black swim trunks, which barely covered anything. Josh did a little jump on the board before he plunged himself into the water. When he climbed out, she clapped.

"Bravo! That's a ten!"

Josh glanced around to see who had called out. When his eyes rested on Angie, he smiled broadly. He walked over to where she was reclining and smiled down at her. She noticed his eyes quickly scan her body.

"Nice to see you again," he said, sweeping his hair back from his face with both hands.

"You, too. Want to sit?"

Josh reached for the next lounge chair and pulled it closer to Angie.

"Nice diving," Angie said, turning her head to the side toward him.

"Thanks, but I'm rusty. Haven't been around a pool, so I need the practice," Josh said, looking over at her.

"Well, you looked pretty good to me," she said. "I don't dive."

"Want to learn?"

"Not really; I'm chicken."

"Umm. So, what do you do?" he asked.

"Travel. I've been traveling a lot this year. But since I'm at my parent's, they said I had to get a job," she said, giving him a scowl. "So, I am now employed at Brian's Burgers. Today is my first day. Woohoo!"

Josh laughed. "Okay. It could be worse."

"I suppose. I'm not used to working. I've been one of those perpetual students." Angie reached for a towel and started blotting herself. "I thought India was hot. Florida could rival that country."

"You've been to India?"

"Yes, it was great," she said. "I lived in several ashrams when I traveled around over there. Amazing experience."

"I've never been in an ashram."

"But you know what one is?"

"Yes. A spiritual place where a guru lives, and you can meditate and do yoga." His expression suggested he wanted her to agree with his definition.

"That's pretty much it," Angie said. "There are spiritual

ceremonies and sat sang, you know, spiritual talks by the guru? Meditation. It's all great."

"So, you're into meditation and gurus?" he asked.

"Oh, sure. It's my passion. I miss the ashram, and the guru," she said. "I came here from an ashram in California. That's pretty much all I've lived in as an adult, except for college dorms."

Josh put his arms behind his head. "I've never experienced any of that. Not even the dorms," he said.

"Really? You didn't go to college?" she asked.

"Nope. I went into business with my father. Wasn't any need to go to college," he said.

"Oh. I thought everyone went to college."

Josh gave her a peculiar look. "No more than everyone lives in an ashram."

Angie wondered if he thought she was spoiled, so she changed the subject. "So, what do you do when you aren't diving off boards?"

"I work. My father travels a lot, so I handle business here when he's gone."

"You don't get to travel with him? Or alone?"

"Rarely. That's not my job."

"Oh." Angie couldn't understand why he didn't seem to want to travel. She loved to travel. "So, you're living here in a condo?"

"For now. When dad travels, I'll be here." He kept his eyes trained forward as he talked.

"When he's here, where will you be?"

"At another condo doing business."

"Another condo? You have more than one?"

"Dad has condos all over. I go to whichever one needs me."

"Oh." Angie contemplated that a bit. "Why would they need you?"

"That's confidential," he said, shifting his position.

"Confidential? Okay, whatever." Angie thought she'd better give up on that line of conversation. Josh did not seem interested in discussing his job.

"I don't mean to be rude, but it's confidential, that's all." Josh closed his eyes.

"It's okay. I don't need to know," Angie said. "What time is it?"

"Not exactly sure, but it has to be after twelve," Josh said.

"Ooh, I'd better go," Angie said, sitting up. "I have to get ready for work."

"Yeah, better not be late on your first day," he said, opening his eyes and studying Angie as she rose with her towel in hand.

"Maybe we can go out some time?" he asked before he lost his opportunity.

Angie smiled at Josh. "I'd like that."

"I'll get with you."

"Okay," she said.

Angie walked away, knowing Josh was studying her as she had studied him earlier.

SEVEN

JOE STOOD in the parking lot and noticed a man he didn't recognize entering the elevator area after being buzzed in. He followed to see which floor the man got off. He was interested to see that the man went into Eneida's old unit. Joe walked toward Rachel's office to give a report. He sat in the prissy chair she had for visitors. He never liked the chair because it was uncomfortable but recognized its value to encourage short visits.

"Hey, Joe."

"Hey," he said, as he pulled out a cloth from his pocket to wipe perspiration from the top of his balding head. "I just saw the new resident for 810. He rode up the elevator."

"Oh? What did he look like?" Rachel asked, curious about the man.

"Well, you thought I was bald," Joe said with a grin, "this guy is a chrome dome. Not a hair on his whole head."

"Really?"

"Yeah. No facial hair, either."

"What was he wearing?"

"A light-colored suit, and a tie."

"Hmm. Must not be from Florida," Rachel said. "It may be winter, but it's still warm here."

"That's what I thought. He was carrying a briefcase, too."

"He's supposed to be a businessman. Interesting."

"Anything happening? Anybody need maintenance today?" he asked. Joe did all the maintenance for the condo. It was a good arrangement since Joe liked to keep busy.

"No, but something odd did happen," Rachel said. "I was going over the security tape to see if anything looked out of place, and guess what I saw?"

"No clue, what?"

"Remember the man seen a while back wearing a long coat and a hat? He was trying to enter, but couldn't get buzzed in and somebody thought he looked suspicious?" Rachel said while rummaging through a pile of papers.

"Sure. We all thought it odd because no one dresses like that in Florida," Joe said. "Especially in the summer months."

"Well, he made a return visit." Rachel fished the photo from the paper pile and handed a picture of a man to Joe. The man was dressed in what looked like an overcoat and a hat.

"He was trying to enter again, like before," she continued. "So, I printed off a picture. The last time we didn't have security cameras."

"I'll be," Joe said, looking at the picture. "He looks shady."

"Doesn't he? I thought so, too." Rachel was glad Joe agreed.

"What are you going to do?"

"I thought I'd give a copy to Detective France. We notified him of this man when he came around the first time. We all thought he had ties to the mob and Loretta, remember?" Rachel said, taking the picture back from Joe.

"Yeah, I remember," Joe said. "Wouldn't hurt to do that. I wonder who he is and why he keeps coming around?"

"I don't know. But if it has to do with a failed attempt on Loretta's life, the police need to know he's back."

"Maybe it's a good thing she's in the hospital?"

"Maybe," Rachel agreed, turning her attention toward the door as it was opening. In walked the new resident.

"Hello, Mr. Brigham," Rachel said, rising from her chair to shake his hand. "I am Rachel; we talked on the phone. This is my husband Joe."

Joe stood to shake the man's hand, then offered him the seat, which he took.

"I thought I should introduce myself, but you already seem to know who I am," Mr. Brigham said. "You can call me John."

"Well, John, my husband saw you entering your condo," she explained, "so, it was easy to determine you were the new owner."

"Thank goodness Josh was home to let me in," he said. "I don't have a key yet."

"Is everything okay with the unit?" Rachel asked.

"Perfectly fine. Josh will be staying there from time to time when I travel," John said. "Maybe in between some. Charles, your condo president, assured me that wouldn't be a problem."

"As long as this isn't his permanent home, it should be all right," she said.

"Good," John said, standing. "Nice to have met you, Rachel — and Joe."

John turned to leave, passing LuAnn on the way out the door.

"Hi, y'all!" LuAnn bustled into the office, wearing a long, fiery orange dress.

"Well, don't you look cool!" Rachel said. She was wearing something similar, but in a dark shade of blue.

"So do you! We should go shopping together more often," LuAnn said, and sat in the chair.

"That's my cue to leave," he said, moving toward the door. "I only stayed because of Mr. Brigham being here."

"I'm glad you did, Joe," Rachel said, smiling at him. "See you at home."

When Joe had left the office, LuAnn asked, "What did you think of Derks?"

"Oh, LuAnn, he's wonderful," Rachel said.

"Isn't he though?"

"I was very impressed with him. He is so gentlemanly, caring, talented – and he's handsome," Rachel said. "You two look like you belong together. Two blonds. You make a handsome couple."

"Oh, I am so tickled you like him. I really, really like him," LuAnn said. "I hope this works out."

"So do I."

"The Brass Rail likes us, too. They are so impressed with the crowds we are drawing, they have extended our stay," LuAnn said, flinging her hand up for emphasis.

Rachel couldn't help but notice the orange polish Lu Anne wore on her nails. Rachel considered the length of LuAnn's nails to be claw-like. How the woman managed to do anything with her hands, she couldn't imagine. Tying a simple shoelace must be impossible for her.

"That's really good news, LuAnn," Rachel said. "That means you will continue performing together."

"Yes, it does, but I think that would have happened anyway," LuAnn said. "The band wants to keep me as their main vocalist. So, wherever they go, I'll be there, too."

"LuAnn, life just keeps getting better for you."

Tears sprang into LuAnn's eyes. "Oh, my false eyelashes are going to come off," she said, waving both her hands in front of her eyes. "But I just can't help crying. It's been so long since something good was happening. God is so good to me."

"I'll say. You are on a positive roll for sure," Rachel said. "I am so happy for you, my friend."

"Thank you."

Rachel was relaxing on the balcony after she attended a Bible study class. She had enjoyed the speaker a lot and felt renewed again. As she sat in her comfy chair, she allowed her eyes to wander. In doing so, she caught sight of a strange scene near the pool area. A couple was walking, hand in hand, in the garden area next to the pool. But it wasn't just any couple.

Rachel stood up, placing her hands on the railing as she gawked at the couple.

"It can't be!" she said aloud.

Four floors below her, Rachel saw Penelope and Alfred holding hands as they walked in the garden. Penelope and Alfred! Every once in a while, one or the other looked adoringly at the other. Rachel was flabbergasted. The two elders were quite opposite in character. Alfred had been married and divorced four times and reportedly had children, although Rachel had never seen any come to visit the old guy. On the other hand, Penelope was a very proper spinster. For all Rachel knew, Penelope had never fallen in love. What an odd pairing.

Joe entered the condo, and Rufus ran from being at Rachel's feet to greet him.

"Good, Rufus! You didn't jump." Joe patted his head in praise.

"Joe, come over here and look," Rachel called out.

"What's happening? Somebody doing cannonballs off the diving board?" he asked.

"No. Look," Rachel said, pointing downward at Penelope and Alfred.

"I'll be darned," Joe said, standing next to Rachel. "The odd couple."

"You've got that right."

They watched as Penelope clutched her sweater closer to her body with one hand, the other still clasped in Alfred's hand.

"How did that happen?" Joe asked.

"I couldn't begin to guess. I've seen them together, but never holding hands. I thought they were just friends."

"A senior romance," Joe said. "Sweet."

Rachel looked at her husband as she considered his statement. "I guess so."

"There's certainly no harm in it."

"I guess not. Just peculiar, the two of them in particular."

They heard the front door close behind them as Angie entered. Rufus promptly greeted her with a wagging tail and droopy tongue.

"Hey, we're over here," Rachel called out.

Angie approached the balcony, trying not to trip over Rufus' eagerness.

"How was work?" Joe asked, sitting in one of the chairs.

"Short day, just training," Angie said, sitting in another chair.

"But did you like it?" Rachel asked, already comfortable in her chair again.

"Too soon to know. But I can see it's going to be rough on my feet," she said. "All the floors are tiled. And it's hot back in the kitchen. Sheesh, is it ever *hot.*"

"It's a kitchen, Angie," Joe reminded her. "It's going to be hot."

"Well, it is. And dirty. Not dirty as in filth, but greasy and food garbage is everywhere," Angie said, releasing her ponytail at the top of her head and then bringing a swath of it under her nose. "I need another shower. My hair smells like grease."

Rachel looked over at her husband, wondering how long Angie would hold her new job. He returned her look, obviously having the same thought.

"Go shower and I'll start dinner." Rachel rose from the chair, glancing down at her daughter. "I'm proud of you for getting a job."

Angie looked up at her mother and smiled softly. "It's nice to hear you're proud of me."

Rachel patted the top of her head affectionately and moved inside.

Angie followed, walking into the hallway toward the bathroom, closing the door behind. Except the latch didn't quite catch. While Angie was in the shower, Precious started playing with the ajar door with her paw. Being a smart cat, she drew the door open and walked out into freedom. Looking around, Precious saw Bennie in the kitchen with Rachel. Bennie caught eyes with Precious and began to growl. Precious let out a hiss.

"What's the matter, Benny?" Rachel said, reaching to stroke the cat. "It's not dinner time yet."

Benny continued to growl while Precious made her way into the living area to investigate. She jumped on top of the sofa after taking a moment to sharpen her claws on its surface. Feeling satisfied, she looked out at the balcony. Bennie left the kitchen in pursuit of Precious. When Bennie sat himself in front of the sofa, growling, Precious spit twice at him. The spitting and growling were heard by Joe and also brought Rachel out of the kitchen. Seeing the situation, she quickly moved into action, as did Rufus. He began to bark at the two cats in their standoff positions.

Joe quickly entered the living room from the balcony. "Hey, cats. No!" He grabbed Rufus' collar to contain him.

Rachel yelled for Angie, then realized she was in the shower and couldn't hear.

"Okay, you little hussy," she said, waving her hands to scare the cat away. "Get back in your room!"

Precious made a run for it, planning to leap from the far edge of the sofa where Rufus stood. But Rufus barked in her face, so she took an angry swat at the dog. After the freshly sharpened claws connected with Rufus' face, he whined, and Joe pulled him away. Precious ran back into the hallway, around the corner, and straight underneath the bed. Benny gave chase until he reached the hallway and then decided he'd had enough. Flicking his tail, Benny turned around and wandered back to the kitchen, suggesting, in his mind, he had defeated the enemy.

Rachel closed the door behind Precious and scolded Benny, as if he could understand her. She threw up her hands in despair then resumed chopping celery. Joe peeked his head around the corner of the kitchen.

"Just a little excitement."

"Um, I could do with less," she said.

"Rufus and I are going for a walk before dinner," he said, attaching a leash to the dog's collar.

"You have plenty of time, don't rush. Oh, and by the way, Rufus needs a bath. He's stinking up the condo."

"Okay, I hear you. Maybe tomorrow."

EIGHT

ANGIE SWEPT THE DISHES, silverware, and cups from the table into the plastic bin and hauled them off to the kitchen. This was a heavy load, so she was careful not to step in grease or a stray onion peel on the floor. She had already taken a tumble due to sliding on grease. Since then, she always wore rubber soled shoes.

"Want me to get these in the dishwasher?" she asked the tall man next to her.

Brian was a big guy, both in height and girth. Since he wasn't presently cooking, he didn't have a hat or hairnet covering his short brown hair. Angie thought her boss ate too many of his burgers. And fries. But he was a decent man to work for, and not bad looking. Clean shaven with even features, his age she guessed to be thirty. His full name printed on the occupational license hanging on the wall was Brian Forbes.

"No, they can wait," Brian said. "Your favorite customer is out there."

"Oh?"

Angie wiped her hands on the white apron covering the

pink waitress uniform as she walked through the swinging doors to the dining room. Mr. Big Tipper was seated in her station, looking at the menu.

"Hi. What can I get you today?" she asked, smiling at the man seated in the red booth.

"Angie, you look lovely today," he said, giving her an approving look. "How about I take you?"

Angie laughed and pushed off the inappropriate remark. "The Burger Bonanza is the special. Want to try that?"

"I think I'd rather try you," he said through a mouth full of smiling teeth.

Again, Angie laughed nervously and tried to get him to place an order. She went through this every day he came in. And that was a lot. This situation had gone beyond flirting into downright annoying.

"Seriously, what would you like to order?" she said, standing with her pen poised to write on the tablet in her hand.

"Well, if you insist," he said. "Just the regular burger and fries."

"Slaw?"

"Yes. You know that's my favorite. And a diet soda."

"Got it," she said, and turned quickly to leave before he could say anything else.

Angie clipped the paper to a round metal apparatus that held the orders and spun around so the cook could read it from the other side of the pass through. Since it was slow, she entered the kitchen and started loading dishes into the washer.

"Still flirting?" Brian asked.

"Yes. He's a creep. As if I'd be interested in him."

The man was middle aged, had prematurely white hair and was nice looking, but definitely an annoyance. Ever since she had started working there, he had taken an interest, always sitting in her section. The diner's layout was three double rows of red booths on the right side of the door, single booths lining the front, side and back, with red topped tables in between that section of booths. The double doors to the kitchen aligned with the front door, with the pass through to the right and waitstaff area that held dishes and utensils. The two booths against the wall on the right were more secluded than the rest of the diner, so that is where he always sat.

Angie felt very uncomfortable around him. His compliments were endless and his intentions obvious. But she was handling the unwanted attention well, she thought. And Brian was aware.

When the cook-in-training slapped the bell to signal her order was ready, Angie quickly grabbed the plate and a can of soda. As she carried the food to the booth, she pasted on her smile. Since he was seated with his back to the wall, he could watch her every step as she came toward him. He smiled as she approached, scanning her body with his eyes.

"Darling, you work too hard," he said, taking the can from her hands. "I could make life easier for you. Why don't you let me?"

This was a new level. He had never been this bold, and Angie was not prepared with a snappy comeback. Living in ashrams had not acquainted her with lecherous men. All the men she met were into peace and love. Her face took on a look of surprise. She was speechless.

"Here, let me take the plate," he said, relieving Angie of the plate in her hand, then clasping that hand in his. He brought her hand up to his face and kissed it. Angie quickly withdrew it.

"Angie, dear, don't be afraid," he said, his blue eyes looking warmly at her. "I don't bite. But I do bring gifts."

The man reached for Angie's arm and drew her closer so

he could pull her to sit beside him. "I have something for you," he said, reaching with the other hand for a small box on the seat next to him. "This is for you, Angie."

He placed the box in her hand. "Open it."

Angie looked at the man's face, not sure how to respond.

"Go ahead. It's all right, really."

Angie opened the white, unwrapped box. Sitting in the middle of a puff of cotton was a silver bangle. It was wide and daintily engraved with leaves and attaching vines. She looked at the man, quizzically.

"Put it on. Go on, Angie."

Angie slipped the bracelet over her hand and looked at its beauty sitting on her wrist. It truly was pretty, and it fit perfectly.

"I, I can't, this is too expensive and…"

"It's nothing like what I can give you, Angie dear. It's just a bauble. A little token of my appreciation for your services."

"No, you see, it wouldn't be right." She was grappling for words. "I hardly know you. I don't even know your name."

"James. My name is James Marshall," he said. "Now, we've been properly introduced."

Angie took a deep breath and released it. "Okay, James. Here's the deal: I don't know you. I don't know that I want to know you, understand? This, this bracelet, is beautiful. Thank you, but I can't accept it. I just can't."

She stood before he could speak. James reached out, grasping her wrist. "I will not accept it back, do *you* understand? I can afford to give you that little bracelet, and far more for that matter. I'm glad you think it's pretty. It's only the beginning of what I'm planning to give you. Just the beginning." He released her wrist. "Now, go do your little job. I would like to eat before this gets cold."

Angie stood silently for two heartbeats, staring at James as he flipped the napkin open, then she walked away. Once inside the kitchen, she decided to hide there until he left. After a while, Brian came over to where she stood peeking out the window of the pass through, looking at James.

"What's going on?"

"I don't know. I don't understand." She turned toward Brian, sticking her arm out. "Look. James gave me this."

"James?"

"He said his name is James. And he gave me this bracelet."

Brian examined the bracelet with his fingers. "Looks like high quality. And expensive."

"I know. He said it was a gift," she said. "A gift?"

One of the other servers came over to inspect the bracelet. Sara Anderson spun it around Angie's wrist as she looked it over. "Man's got good taste," Sara said. "Keep it."

"Did I do something to make him think he could give me this?" she asked Brian.

"Probably not. Maybe he's just real generous," he said. "Or he has the hots for you."

"I don't want him to have the hots for me," Angie said. "He's old enough to be my father."

"A sugar daddy is what that's called," Sara said, winking. "You have been blessed."

Angie gave Sara a horrified look.

"Well, 'James' just left," Brian said. "I saw him walk out. Go see if he paid for his meal."

Angie walked out the kitchen and over to the booth where James had been. Among the dirty dishes was a hundred-dollar bill. He had more than paid for his meal.

Ruby entered Rachel's office while she was looking over the security tape.

"Whatcha doing?" Ruby asked, sitting in the chair in front of the desk.

"Looking over the security tape," she said, turning to Ruby. "I have a new job duty… viewing activities during the night. Anyone who tries to enter or do something stupid, I can see it recorded on the tape."

"See anything interesting?"

"Yes, look," Rachel turned the screen toward Ruby. "That's the mystery man who keeps coming around for who knows what reason."

Ruby saw a man, dressed in a long coat and a hat. "Isn't that the guy from last year? You mean he's back?"

"I'm afraid so. I don't know why, but he's visited us twice before this."

"Can you blow that up bigger?" Ruby asked.

"Sure," Rachel said, thinking Ruby's eyes must be getting weaker. "Can you see him better?"

"Sure can. He looks familiar."

"What?" Rachel didn't expect to hear that.

"Yeah, the way he stands is odd and familiar, like someone I once knew."

"Really? All this time I thought maybe it was someone looking for Loretta," she said. "Since she was once a high-profile detective, who knows who might want to seek revenge?"

"That's true, but he looks familiar to me," Ruby said, intently looking at the screen while rubbing her chin. "Be nice to see his face clearly, but that dumb hat he's wearing casts shadows."

"Well, think about it, Ruby. Maybe it will come to you," she said. "So, what brings you here today?"

"Loretta," she said with a sigh. "They've got her on oxygen. She looks poorly. She's so weak, and she doesn't want to eat. They've got her all drugged up, but she's not improving. I am so worried about her."

"I am so sorry," she said. "What can I do?"

"Say prayers. Aren't you supposed to be religious or something? Don't you go to church?"

"Yes, I go to the same church as Loretta."

"Well, then, pray for the woman."

"I will, Ruby. Can I pray for you, too?"

"Sure, why not? I can always use a little boost in that department." The old lady smiled, accentuating the wrinkles around her eyes.

Rachel smiled, too, at the words spoken. It wasn't long ago that this conversation would not have taken place. She hadn't attended church since childhood and was pursuing a personal path to destruction. Her marriage was at stake because her husband had an incorrect conception of her odd behavior, causing her to become defiant and rebellious. It had been the worst time in her life. But she got through it, with the help of God.

"Is she up for visitors?" Rachel was eager to visit the woman.

"Yeah, but don't expect a lot from her. You'll have to do most of the talking."

"I can do that. Thank you for telling me about her."

"I'll keep you informed," she said, rising from the chair. "Just pray for her."

"Consider it done."

NINE

LUANN WAS the first to arrive at the clubhouse, so she chose the table. Olivia Washington followed close behind, and then Rachel arrived. This was a convenient place for them to have their chats and catch up on each other's life. A circular bar was in the center of the room with tables dispersed around. Located on the same level as Rachel's office, it also provided a gathering place for special events the residents might want to host.

"I cannot wait for the summer break," Olivia said as she sat in a chair. "These kids are killing me this semester."

"I thought college kids were supposed to be easier than high school," LuAnn said. "Of course, there are the parties and all that craziness, but they're supposed to be studying for their careers."

"You would think so, wouldn't you? But this bunch seem to have torture on their agendas. My torture." Olivia wagged her head in disgust as she adjusted in her chair.

"How so?" Rachel asked.

"They try my patience by being late," Olivia said, checking

her curly wig with her fingers to see if it was still in place. "And then they take forever to get settled. Once they're settled, they talk to each other like I'm invisible. They act like they're in their dorms. No respect shown."

"Rude," Rachel said.

"Ladies?" The server arrived at their table.

"Iced tea for me," Rachel said.

"Draft," said LuAnn.

"Diet soda," Olivia said and continued. "This is the rudest bunch of students I have ever taught since I've been at Bethune Cookman."

Olivia Washington was a professor by trade and a gentle heart by nature. While raising four kids as a single mom, she put herself through college so she could provide a better life for her children. Once they were on their own, Olivia sold the house she and her husband had owned before he passed away and moved to the condo.

"Not to ignore your drama, but I heard from Tia today," Rachel said.

"Oh, I've had her on my mind. How is she?" asked Olivia.

"So far, she likes being back in India," Rachel said. "She didn't think she would, but her parents need her now, so she has no choice."

"Is she staying with them?" LuAnn asked.

"For now. She's figuring out if they need round the clock care or just while she works."

"I hope she doesn't regret returning home," Olivia said, fingering the white collar next to her cocoa hued skin. "She is so Americanized; it could be difficult."

"She doesn't have any choice. Her father is in a wheelchair and her mother has several illnesses," Rachel said. "Family first. It's also helpful that she's a doctor."

"It doesn't sound like she'll be moving to her own place," LuAnn said, drumming her pink nails on the table.

"I doubt it, too," Rachel said.

The server returned with their drinks. Once he left, they resumed their conversation.

"How is Angie doing at her job?" Olivia asked.

"Really well. I'm surprised," Rachel said. "She likes her boss, and apparently she's doing decent as a server considering she's never done anything like that before. She's never had a job."

"Good for her," LuAnn said. "Tell her I'm proud of her."

"I will. She has a date with the son of our newest tenant," Rachel said, stirring her tea with the straw. "So, maybe she'll have a romance besides her job."

"I haven't met him, but I saw him at a distance," Olivia said. "He's really good looking."

"I know. She calls him the hunk."

"He is pretty hunky," LuAnn agreed, adjusting the straps on her blue top. "If I were her age, I'd tackle him for sure. He says hi every time we meet on the walkway."

"Lucky you, he's your next-door neighbor," Olivia said.

Alfred and Penelope entered the clubhouse, hand in hand. They looked around for an empty table. Spotting one near the girls, Penelope pulled Alfred behind her to the table. He pulled the heavy chair out for her and then sat next to Penelope.

"I wonder what they drink?" LuAnn said.

"A Shirley Temple for Penelope," Rachel said, and they all giggled.

The server went over, and they eavesdropped to hear the order.

"A draft for me," Alfred said, "and a Shirley Temple for the lady."

Rachel smacked her hand against her mouth to silence her laugh. Olivia turned her smirking face away while

LuAnn let it rip. Her laugh rang out, causing numerous people to stare at her.

"Sorry," she called out to everyone. "Funny joke."

"On that note, I need to get to some paperwork," Olivia said, grinning as she rose. "I'll see you two later in the week."

"I should go, too," Rachel said, standing. "Joe might still be awake."

"Aw, my night off and you're leaving," LuAnn said, sticking her pink lips out in a pout.

"I'm still making things up to Joe after all those nights I stayed out so late with you girls," Rachel said, slinging her bag over her shoulder. "Now when I come home, he's eager to see me. And that crazy dog has stopped attacking me since Angie arrived."

"That's great, honey. Say hi to Joe for me," LuAnn said.

"See ya later."

"Bye."

The sand felt good between her toes. It was cold and wet as Angie stepped over shells near the ocean's edge. She carried her sandals in her hand and enjoyed the cool breeze that swept passed her thighs. She had stressed over which shorts to wear for their date, finally choosing the white ones. They showed off what little tan she had. The red top displayed just enough skin without being too revealing. Besides, he'd already seen her in a bikini.

"I love the beach at night," Angie said, kicking a shell.

"Yeah, it's peaceful."

The moon was shooting down beams to light their path while the waves swept in to wash their feet. The rushing sound of the water pulled all the tension of the day from Angie. James had come by the diner again. Nothing had changed. Well-dressed in a blue, short-sleeved shirt, and khaki slacks, he was a determined man. Determined to get Angie to go out with him. He wanted to take care of her. He wanted to buy her things. He wanted...

"I'm leaving town in a couple days," Josh said, breaking into her thoughts.

"Oh? Where are you going?"

"Chicago, then Vegas."

"For business?"

"Yes."

Angie had no intention of asking what he was going to do there. He'd have to tell her himself. If he would.

"I'll be gone about ten days."

"Well, you know where I'll be."

"At the diner, beating off lecherous old men."

"That sounds funny when you put it that way."

"Hey, he wants to give you jewelry, let him. He gives you big tips, take them. Take anything he gives you. As long as you don't have to give anything in return." Josh added a nod for emphasis.

"I have no intention of giving him what he wants."

Josh stopped walking and reached out for her arm, turning her toward him. "Maybe I should pay him a visit? Have a talk with him."

Angie shook her head and looked down. "That's not necessary. I can handle this."

"You sure? Because I can do it."

"No. He'll get tired of the chase," she said, looking up into his face. "This will be old news by the time you get back."

"Okay," he said, starting to walk again. "You warm enough? It's getting chilly."

Josh was dressed in his signature black. Black tee-shirt and jeans, always black. He reached into a pocket and pulled out a cigarette and lighter, motioning them toward her. With a closer look, Angie saw the twisted end and knew what it was. "Hum?"

"Ah, no, I don't do that."

"No? Never?"

"Well, not never. I tried it once, but I decided it wasn't for me."

"It's good stuff," Josh said, lighting the end. "Try it." He brought his hand closer to her face. "Take a drag."

"Not a good idea, sorry."

They walked along silently while Josh finished smoking.

"The stars seem brighter and bigger," he said. "And the ocean glistens more intensely."

"I think the stars and ocean are beautiful the way they are from my view," she said.

"Doesn't hurt anything," he said, excusing his action.

Angie didn't respond. No point in arguing with him.

They walked back to the condo and rode the elevator to the fourth floor.

"It was nice getting to know you," she said, turning toward him.

"Same here. When I get back, we'll do it again."

"Okay."

Josh slowly leaned in, taking her upper arms in his hands, and gave her a kiss on the cheek. He pulled back a little, holding her gaze, and then kissed her lips gently. Just once. Then he released her arms. "Goodnight."

"Goodnight." Angie turned away and left the elevator.

When she walked through the door of her parent's condo, she was smiling. "Hel-lo," she said as she passed her mother.

"Hello." Rachel gave her a peculiar look. "How was your date?"

"Lovely."

"Lovely?"

"Um hm, lovely. He's lovely, too."

"Okay…"

"Goodnight, mother."

Mother? Since when did Angie call her mother? *That must have been some date.*

TEN

JOSH HAD HIS SUITCASE PACKED. This wouldn't be a long trip. At least he didn't intend it to be. He wanted to get back to continue his pursuit of Angie. She was hot, and a bit naïve, despite all her travels. He didn't mind that. It made for an easier conquest. He was all about conquests. He had looks, charm, and money. He knew how to maneuver women. And he had set his sights on Angie.

His father had already given him directions on how to close three deals he had on the table. Whenever he was sent out to handle business, it was usually to collect what was owed. John didn't like to be owed anything. He expected timely pay, and if not, well, Josh handled the details. He never asked how, just anticipate the job would get done. And it always did. Josh was good at his job.

"Want me to drop you at the airport?" John entered the bedroom Josh was to occupy when there. "It's only about four miles from here, which is nice. Especially compared to some of the other cities."

"I was going to get a cab, but if you want to drop me, that's fine."

"Sure. You ready?"

"Yeah, I am."

"Let's go." John walked out of the bedroom, jiggling the car keys in his pocket.

As they rode down the elevator, Josh looked over at his father. He respected him greatly. After his mother died, it became the two of them. While his father wasn't a loving man, Josh always knew he would be cared for and safe. When he traveled, there were men around for protection and women who came in to cook and clean at the condos. He never had to fend for himself; his dad saw to his every need. Despite the older man's lack of warmth, Josh knew he could talk to his father about anything. All he had to do was ask. He frequently received worldly advice about how to survive in a dog eat dog world. His father was more than a father, he was a mentor.

After they got in the car, John gave his son some last-minute instructions.

"Frank is an okay dude, but you have to watch out for Al. He's quiet. Too quiet. I don't trust him." John kept his eyes on the road as he drove.

"Okay."

"When he gives you the money, don't linger. Leave immediately," he said, making a left turn at the light. "You better meet at a public place. Avoid a private meet. Not safe."

"Okay. I met him before, didn't I?" he asked, keeping his eyes straight ahead toward the road as well.

"Just once, but not there. In Jersey."

"Right."

"You have the cell numbers?"

Josh looked over at his dad. "Of course. This isn't my first time."

"Yeah. Sorry," he said. "I'm just anxious to clear this up. This has been an outstanding debt for too long."

"Don't worry about it. I've got it covered."

They pulled to the curb in front of the Delta Airlines entrance. While a wide selection of airlines was not offered, the convenience of coming and going from the Daytona Beach Airport made up for that. There was never a hassle during check in or long lines passing through security like at the larger airports. Josh jumped out, opened the backdoor and grabbed his suitcase. Before he shut the door, he said, "I'll call when the deal is done. Later."

John pulled away from the curb without a word.

Brian's Burgers was hopping. A large portion of the motorcycle crowd visiting Daytona Beach was filling the booths on a regular basis. Doctors, lawyers, mechanics, and John Doe-from-anywhere-America were gathered for Bike Week. One just had to love riding motorcycles and desire a vacation with like-minded folks to come to Daytona Beach. And they were welcomed. When Bikers roared into town, it meant merchants prospered and restaurants reaped big dollars. Bikers were good tippers, too.

Angie was running back and forth from the kitchen to the dining room as fast as she could move. Her tips had been great, and she was appreciative, although very tired at night when she arrived home. As she passed one table while carrying a full load of dirty dishes in her plastic bin, a hand reached out and grabbed her arm.

"Angie."

She looked to see who called her by name and saw that it was James. He was sitting alone at a small table, probably because all the booths were taken.

"You're not in my section," she said. "I can't wait on you."

"Can you make an exception?"

"No, I can't. Those are the rules."

"How about meeting me when you get off work?"

Angie felt her entire body slump. "James, I can't. I will be too tired."

"But…"

Angie abruptly jerked her arm from his grasp as she walked toward the kitchen. *Maybe he will take the hint?* When she returned after dumping the dishes, she found him placing his order with Sara. She was going overboard with broad smiles and sashaying her hips from side to side as she wrote the order in her tablet. *Good!* Sara was more his age.

Another bunch of bikers occupied a six-spot table in her section. "Hi, guys," she said, smiling. "What's your pleasure this evening?"

"Well, if I can't have you, I'll take the burger special," said one of the men, matching her smile. "And a Coke."

"You're going to love it," she said, still smiling. "We're famous for our burger specials."

The other five gave their orders, then she walked to the pass through to clip the order to the metal holder. From the corner of her eye, she saw James staring at her. She wished he'd just give it up and not return to the restaurant. Why couldn't he understand she wasn't interested?

As the night wore on and her feet hurt more, Angie noticed James had finally left. He'd dawdled around long enough to irritate Sara, finally leaving her a decent tip, but not a hundred-dollar bill. She hoped Sara didn't blame her.

When ten o'clock rolled around, the diner was empty, and the staff was preparing to clean up and leave. Angie thought that if her feet could talk, they would have her arrested for abuse. She made quick work of her clean up duties and left by the back door. It felt good to feel the cool ocean breeze sweep over her face after a long day. Oh, the joy of just walking quietly home. She removed her shoes so the sand could comfort her feet. It was only three blocks down the beach to the condo. This little walk was definitely the best part of her day.

Angie saw lots of people walking on the beach. Some were going to clubs or restaurants, others, who knew where? Each was dressed differently. Some were in shorts, others in sun dresses, and still others in jeans. An eclectic display of people enjoying an evening on the beach. She heard a band playing as she passed a honkytonk bar, the music and laughter spilling from the open door. A Ferris wheel was ahead, brightly lit as it moved the screaming passengers around. As she walked, Angie became aware of a car driving slowly beside her. She glanced over and quickly recognized the driver. It was James. She pulled herself upright in alert mode. What did he think he was doing? The window slid down and he smiled at her.

Angie frowned at the man in response. "What are you doing? I'm off duty."

"Why don't you get in my car?" he asked pleasantly. "I'll take you home, unless you want to go somewhere else first?"

His vehicle was an expensive SUV, dark metallic green in color. Maybe a Lincoln, she wasn't sure.

"I do not want to go somewhere with you. I am *not* getting in your car, James."

"You shouldn't have to walk home when I can easily take you." James gave her a charming smile. "Come on, Angie."

"That is not your problem, how I get home. You should mind your own business and not step into mine. You are *not* taking me home. Understand?" Angie's voice had risen a couple decibels in an effort to make her point. "Get out of here!"

"I understand, but you don't understand my intentions." James wasn't giving up easily.

"Oh, I totally understand your intentions, James. Leave me alone!" She shouted the last sentence at the man.

About that time, two biker types were walking nearby, probably having left the honkytonk. The men stopped to observe the exchange between the young woman and the older man. As luck would have it, Angie had waited on these two men from the six-spot table earlier that evening.

"Hey, you okay, Angie?" one asked as they approached her from behind.

"Yeah, we're here if you need help," said the other.

Both men were formidable in size, had beards, and wore skull caps. They leaned their muscular bodies from one side to the other as they made their presence known, indicating they were ready to step in to defend a damsel in distress.

"Uh, well…" Angie said, taking several backward steps toward the men. "That depends." She cocked her head to the side as she stood silently rooted in the sand in front of the two burly men as James decided what he wanted to do. She hoped her body language and that of the two bikers suggested to James that he might want to move along. James decided wisely. He drove off down the beach.

Angie turned around to face the two men who had come to her defense. "Thanks, guys. I don't get this dude. He keeps coming into the diner and bothering me. He doesn't take no for an answer. And tonight, he's trying to take me home. But thank you so much."

"It's okay. If you ever need us, we're here for you," said one of the men.

"I really appreciate that."

"Are you walking far?" asked the other man.

"No, just another block or so."

"Why don't we walk with you? Make sure you're safe."

"That would be great."

The two men accompanied Angie, walking on either side of her, as they safely escorted her to the condo and watched as she entered the building. She waved at them once inside.

Angie punched the fourth-floor button and rode up the elevator, feeling like someone or something had been watching over her. Those guys were sent to her aid.

When she entered her parent's unit, she found them in the living room, reading.

"Hi, honey," called out Rachel.

"Hey," said her dad.

"How was work?" her mother asked.

"Extremely busy," Angie said. "The bikers are in town, so we were swamped."

"Always good business from the bikers," Joe said.

"And tips. They're known for tipping well," Rachel said.

"Yeah, well, there's this older man who tips really well, too," she said, tossing her purse on the table. "He comes in regularly and has the hots for me. He was there tonight. Again."

"Was he inappropriate?" Joe asked.

"Yes, but there were a lot of people around. But tonight, he drove by me on the beach when I was coming home. He wanted me to get in his car."

"*What?*" Joe looked like he was ready to explode.

"You shouldn't walk home at night," Rachel said. "That's just asking for trouble."

"Well, I've done it before without a problem, but tonight he found me." She flounced into one of the chairs. "Two bikers I had waited on earlier came to my rescue. They walked me home."

"Bless them for that," Joe said.

"I don't know what to do about this guy. He wants to give me things and says he wants to take care of me. I mean, really?" She looked to her parents for an answer. "He gave me a silver bracelet. How crazy is that?"

"He's a nut job and you need to stay away from him," Joe

said, looking flushed over his daughter's encounter. "Tell Brian to handle it."

"Yes, Brian should step in and do something, Angie," her mother said. "This can't continue, you have to ask him for help."

"I will."

ELEVEN

LORETTA'S FACE was so pale, it almost blended with the white pillowcase her head lay on. She was lying on her back breathing with the aid of the oxygen machine when Rachel entered her room at the hospital. She wasn't sure if Loretta was asleep or not until she sat in the chair beside the bed. Loretta's eyes flipped open immediately.

"Rachel, dear," Loretta whispered, after moving the oxygen cup to the side. Her eyes smiled, but her mouth didn't respond.

"Loretta, hi," Rachel said, taking one of the old lady's hands into her own. "Don't strain yourself to talk."

Loretta slid the cup back in place, struggling to take a deep breath.

"Okay, so, nothing has changed much at the condo since you've been here," Rachel said, trying to entertain the woman. "Oh, you did know Alfred and Penelope are an item?"

Loretta gave one nod of her head.

"That is such a strange coupling, don't you think? Penelope is such a prudish woman, and here her boyfriend has been married and divorced four times. I guess you'd call him a boyfriend, right? They do hold hands." Rachel just yammered on, hoping the old woman was enjoying her chatter. "At their age, I can't imagine anything intimate happening, can you?"

Loretta gave a slight sideways wag of her head. She kept looking up at Rachel, her eyes full of appreciation.

A nurse came in the room. "Are you her daughter?"

"No, just a close friend."

"You two looked like you were bonded in some way."

Rachel gazed at the old woman lying in the bed as she still held her hand. "We are. She's very special to me."

"I have to take her down for some tests," the nurse announced. "I'm sorry."

"That's okay. I can always return." Rachel stood and released Loretta's hand gently to the bed. "I'll come back soon. I'm sure Ruby will be here later."

The old woman gave one nod of her head.

"Bye, Loretta. Behave yourself."

"You have to do something, Brian."

The man looked at Angie with reluctance in his eyes. It was obvious that he did not relish speaking to a customer about their inappropriate behavior with one of his wait staff.

"He's ignoring my protests to leave me alone. You can't allow this to continue. It's not right."

Brian wiped his hand down his face and sighed. "Okay. If he comes in, tell me."

Several hours later, Angie saw James enter the diner and take a seat at one of the back booths. As soon as she had finished bussing the table, she lugged the plastic bin full of dishes back into the kitchen.

"Brian," she called out. "He's here."

Her boss turned away from the grill, placing the long-handled spatula on the stainless steel counter. "Got it."

For all of his girth and height, Brian was a wimp. He did not like confrontation, and least of all with a customer. He was a Christian and tried to express love, not anger. Taking a deep breath, he left the kitchen through a swinging door on the right side. That was the rule: only use the right side, no matter which approach you came by. He walked over to where James was seated and sat across from him at the table.

"Hello, Brian," James said casually.

"Yeah, James, I need to talk with you."

"Certainly."

"You have to leave my staff alone, man. I can't have customers hitting on my girls."

"Who said I'm hitting on your girls?" He gave Brian an innocent look.

"You know what I'm talking about. Buying gifts, being pushy. It has to stop." Brian dug his eyes into the older man, not blinking.

James quickly licked his lips and tilted his head. "I'm not sure what you mean."

"Man, you know exactly what I'm saying," Brian said, rubbing one hand over his head, pausing at the back of his neck. "Leave Angie alone or I'll have to ask you to stop coming in."

James did not respond, just stared at Brian.

"One of the other girls will wait on you," Brian continued, standing.

Angie was watching from the kitchen pass through. As soon as Brian re-entered the kitchen, she asked for details.

"I told him to leave you alone and another girl would wait on him."

"And he agreed?"

"He didn't say anything. He also didn't admit to anything."

Angie looked at Brian, questions on her face.

"Just see what happens. He'll probably not come back," Brian said as he walked to the grill. "Bonnie, go wait on him."

The new girl, Bonnie Gibson, quickly headed out the door to wait on James. Maybe he would think Bonnie's bouncy red ponytail was cute. She could only hope. But when Angie approached the table next to James to take a couple's order, she could feel James' eyes boring into her. She felt nervous but was hopeful this would be the last time he came into the diner.

"Where have you been?" Rachel asked as Joe entered their condo. "I lost track of you a couple hours ago."

"I have been on an investment search."

"A what?" Rachel looked up from dusting the coffee table.

"The other day I was driving down Beach Street and noticed a house for sale," Joe said, sitting in one of the chairs. "So, I went back today when they were having an open house."

"A house? We don't need a house, we have this condo."

"I know. This would be for a bed and breakfast or a couple nights' stay for tourists."

Rachel stopped dusting. "A B and B?"

"Why not?"

"I don't know. I never thought about investing that way." Rachel shrugged her shoulders. "What did it look like?"

"Pretty clean, overall. Nothing I couldn't fix up myself, mostly cosmetic."

"Hmm." Rachel sat on the edge of the couch. "And you're seriously considering this for us?"

"Yes."

"When can I see it?"

"How about right now? The open house is still going on, and the place is only over the bridge and to the left a bit. Close by."

Rachel rose to her feet. "I'm ready. Let's go."

The house was a bright yellow, two story Victorian. Overlooking the river across the street, it would be a desirable location for tourists, Rachel thought. Close to entertainment and restaurants on Beach Street, and a quick ride over the bridge to the beach.

"This is an ideal location," Rachel said as she walked up the steps to the wrap around porch. "It's cute."

A man appeared at the front door. "Come on in, folks," he said. "Hello, Joe." The real estate agent opened the door for them.

"This is my wife Rachel," Joe said. "Don is the agent."

They exchanged pleasantries as Rachel and Joe entered the house.

A fairly large living room welcomed them and was nicely staged with antique-looking furniture. The brick fireplace gave a cozy feel to the area. To the left side was an open staircase leading to the second floor. Crown molding decorated the ceiling with the design matching certain areas of the fireplace mantle. Rachel walked through the archway ahead that led to the dining room. Again, staged in antique-looking furniture, Rachel felt she was being taken back in time. To the right side was a doorway to the kitchen. While it wasn't a large kitchen, it held certain qualities that made it feel homey, such as white painted cabinets.

"Do the furnishings come with the house?" Rachel asked.

"Yes, everything you see goes with the sale," Don said.

Rachel and Joe left that area and walked up the staircase to the second floor. There were four bedrooms and one bath, complete with a clawfoot tub.

"Hmm, one bathroom?" Rachel said. "I don't think that's enough if all four bedrooms are occupied by unrelated people."

"No, it's not," Joe said, standing by the tub. "I'd need to add a bathroom."

"Okay, so that's a big-ticket item. Otherwise, paint would be necessary, but that's a small item," she said as she entered one of the bedrooms. "Holy cow, what is that?"

Rachel froze as she stared across the room at the built-in wall unit. Along each of the three shelves was a collection of old dolls. Very old, creepy looking dolls.

"The doll collection. They are included with the sale, too," Don said. "The owner's great grandmother owned the dolls."

"Definitely creepy," Rachel said. "It's like a wall of little faces staring back at us."

Joe chuckled. "Oh, they're cute, Rachel. Loosen up."

Rachel swung her eyes over to Joe. "You've got to be kidding!"

They came downstairs, and Joe excused himself and Rachel so they could talk privately. The couple went out to the porch.

"What do you think?" he asked.

"I think it's a good idea, minus the dolls."

Joe shook his head. "They don't bother me. Ignore that part. What about the rest of the house? I like it."

"Me, too."

"Should we do it?"

"My vote is yes."

Joe walked back into the house. Rachel stayed outside, leaning on the railing as she looked across Beach Street at the river. This was the way they always did things. When it was right, it was right. They always knew. No sense beating the question to death.

"You've got a deal," Joe said to Don.

"Terrific!" Don said, reaching for the paperwork on the table. "All of this needs to be filled out and then we can set a date for the closing."

"Thanks, Don."

"My pleasure, Mr. Barnes."

TWELVE

ANGIE LEFT WORK AT FIVE. She hurried home to grab a shower and dress for her date with Josh. She was anxious to see him, to see what happened this time. To see where this relationship was going. Although it really wasn't a relationship yet.

"Hey," she called out as she walked inside her parents' condo.

No one answered, so she immediately went into her bedroom to get ready. After a shower and shampoo to get the grease smell out of her hair, she quickly blew her hair straight and applied minimal makeup. She stood back from the mirror and approved of her appearance. White slacks, turquoise top, showing a hint of cleavage, real turquoise jewelry on her ears, fingers, and wrist. She didn't know where they were going, only that he said be casual.

"Meow." Precious was weaving between her ankles. "Meow."

"Are you hungry?" Angie shook out some crunchy food into the cat dish. That ended the cat discussion. Precious pounced on the food, swishing her bushy tail in the air as she contentedly munched away.

When she heard the doorbell, Angie walked to the door. Her stomach did a flipflop as she pulled it open.

"Hey, gorgeous."

"Hi."

"Ready?"

"Yes, let me grab my bag." Angie reached behind the door to lift her purse from the doorknob of the storage closet. "Got it."

They silently rode down the elevator. To break the silence, Angie asked where they were going?

"A place on the ocean. A guy I know runs it. Great fish."

"Oh, great. Sounds good."

"My car's over there," he said, pointing in the direction where a Cadillac and Porsche were parked. She wondered which was his.

Josh walked to the passenger side of the ivory Porsche, unlocking and opening the door for her.

Angie dropped into the seat and swung her long legs under the dash. "Nice car."

Josh smiled and shut the door.

Angie carefully looked over the car, trying not to be obvious. It appeared to be a new model. Expensive and extravagant for a young man to drive. She couldn't help think that his father must pay well. *Really* well.

They arrived at a restaurant that looked nice on the outside and shrieked Florida inside with its décor. Conk shells were attached to worn, brown shiplap walls, along with some fish netting. The furnishings were rustic and worn in appearance, likely to have been purposely weathered. Dark wooden tables had white tablecloths and napkins, with one lantern in the center of each table. At the entrance, a large fish tank protruded into the waiting area.

As soon as they entered, they were shown to a table, despite six couples waiting. They were seated by a window that overlooked the ocean's waves crashing onto shore. The view was spectacular. Angie noticed the only bright color in the large dining room was the orange curtains tied back with aqua rope.

The wait staff was all men. One dark haired, mustached young man quickly approached their table. "Good evening. I'm Jerry."

"Hi, Jerry," Angie said. "I wait tables, too."

"Oh, nice. Would you like something to drink?" Jerry hustled along, not taking time for small chat.

"Well, yes, a glass of iced tea."

"Don't you want a real drink?" Josh asked her.

"No, I want iced tea."

"I'll have a vodka martini, dry, rocks, and two olives," Josh said to the server.

They looked at the menu the young man had left for each of them.

Josh looked seriously at her from across the table. "What looks good to you? Anything you want, order it."

"Hmm, I was thinking the tuna steak," she said. It wasn't the most expensive item on the menu, but it wasn't the cheapest, either.

Josh smiled. "A woman after my heart. I love tuna, too. I'll have the same."

The waiter returned with their drinks and took the order for two medium rare tuna steaks.

"How is the job?" he asked.

"Better. I've gotten used to it."

"What about that man harassing you?"

"Brian talked to him today and told him to leave me alone or he'd be asked not to come back," she said, placing her napkin in her lap.

"Good."

"But that was after James tried to get me into his car when I was walking home."

Josh's jaws noticeably tightened in reaction.

"Fortunately, two bikers I had waited on came to my rescue. James left and they walked me the rest of the way home." Angie looked at him, expecting Josh to be pleased to hear everything worked out. But Angie could see that he was agitated.

"You tell me if he comes back and I'll take care of it," he said sternly. "I'm serious."

Angie's eyes widened over his statement. "It's nothing to be concerned about. It's handled."

"And if it's not, let me know," he said.

Angie gave him a little smile and changed the subject. "How was your trip?"

"Busy and stressful at times."

"Oh, why?"

"I hate flying. I hate airports, the crowds, it gets annoying."

"Oh. I love to fly."

"Not me. And dealing with people in business, that's stressful. I'd rather be with you." He took a sip of his drink, looking across the table, and then gave her a big smile. When he did, the dimples in both cheeks flashed out.

"That's sweet. So, now you are." She took a sip of her iced tea.

Josh raised his glass toward her. "A toast: to the most beautiful woman in the room." Angie touched his glass with hers and smiled.

"You do heap on the compliments." It wasn't that she didn't like being complimented; he just laid it on extra thick.

"Only to deserving people."

After more small talk, the server arrived with their tuna steaks, placing the large plates in front of them. The aroma from the tuna made her mouth water. Dinner also included garlic mashed potatoes, asparagus, and dinner rolls. Angie was delighted with her meal.

"How was business, besides being stressful?" Angie asked.

"I deal with jerks. Some are scumbags," he said pricking the side of his tuna with a fork.

Angie blinked at the word scumbag. "Really? How so?"

Josh seemed to catch himself, realizing he was saying too much. He smiled at Angie as he took a bite of tuna. "Oh, you know, some people are overbearing, maybe not as honest as others. Try to con you. And I have to clean up the mess."

"I see." But Angie didn't have a clue what he meant. "What mess?"

Josh sighed as he thought what to say next. Angie could tell. "When someone makes a mess of business, I have to go in and straighten it out. People don't like that."

"Of course."

"So, I think these people are scumbags. Jerks. Lowlifes."

"Okay." It really wasn't okay that he had such a bad opinion of people, but she had to say something.

"How is the tuna?" he asked.

"Fantastic. I love it."

"Good." Josh smiled at Angie again.

As she took a sip of her iced tea, Angie noticed a storm brewing out in the ocean. Bursts of lightning sparked and then died. Such a pretty sight. This should have been the perfect evening, the beginning of two people getting to know each other. But everything changed after this.

"I am so worried about Loretta," Rachel said while stirring the soup she had made from scratch. She always used her mother's heavy pot when making soup. It was sort of an heirloom, or at least to Rachel.

"She's in good hands," Joe said from the chair by the small table in the kitchen. "She'll pull out of this."

"I don't know. She looked terrible, and she's so weak."

"Keep a positive attitude."

"I try, but she is up in age," Rachel said, adding more salt to the pot. She caught the scent of garlic as she stirred. "I am so fond of her."

"I know you are, but I think you're remembering your mother."

Rachel's mother died after she contracted pneumonia when she was in her upper eighties. The similarities were uncanny.

"You could be right," she said, banging the spoon on the side of the pot. "Okay, note to self: knock it off."

Joe smiled at his wife. "Is Angie joining us for dinner?"

"No, she's on a date with Josh."

"Really? Where'd they go?"

"I don't know. He told her to dress casual."

"That could mean anything from a movie to a walk on the beach or dinner at a burger joint."

"I doubt they'll eat at a burger joint after Angie has been working at one all day."

"True. How soon till dinner?"

"Very soon. You can wash your hands, we're almost ready to eat. You could also get out the spoons and knives. We won't need forks," she said.

Joe washed his hands in the bathroom, then pulled out the kitchen drawer that contained the utensils, selecting what she had requested.

"Butter?" he asked.

"Yes. I have bread in the oven."

"I know. I can smell it." Joe placed the spoons and knives on the table in the dining room, then brought the butter from the refrigerator.

Rachel carried the bowls of soup to the table, then went back to get the bread from the oven, placing it in a basket. Both sat at the table and Joe said grace.

"Has Angie been looking for a job?" he asked.

Rachel knew Joe meant a job that paid well. The one she had at the diner was supposed to be temporary. "She hasn't had a lot of time to look since she started at Brian's Burgers," Rachel said, blowing on a spoonful of soup. "She's also tired from the physical work there, so she's not really motivated to get up early on the few days she has to look."

"I can understand that," Joe said, taking a bite of bread. "Ah, this is incredible. Did you put garlic in it, or is that smell coming from the soup?"

"Both."

"Good job."

Rachel reached for her fan and gyrated air into her face. "Every time I eat soup, my hot flashes worsen."

"I thought those were temporary."

"They are, but temporary can mean a couple years."

"Oh."

"Joe?" she looked over at her husband with a question in her eyes. "What do you think of Josh? Is he a good influence for our daughter?"

"He seems okay, I guess. Why? You don't like him?"

"There's nothing to dislike. He's charming, handsome, very polite, but I don't know." She placed the fan on the table.

"Is your intuition kicking in?"

"Maybe. Or maybe it's just a mother's worry."

"Give him some time. If he's not good for Angie, we'll see it."

A flash of lightning tripped across the sky.

"Ooh, another storm," she said, taking her first bite of bread.

"Like clockwork."

"It's Florida."

THIRTEEN

THEY ENTERED UNIT 810. Angie had never been in this unit, before or after the murder.

"I thought you'd be able to meet Dad," Josh said, "but I don't think he's here."

"Another time," Angie said.

"Let's go over there," he said, motioning toward the couch. "Would you like a glass of wine?"

"No, thank you."

Josh turned to the kitchen as Angie made her way to the couch. She glanced around at the furnishings. Decidedly masculine. Black leather furniture, glass tables, a large flat screen TV hung on the wall. Otherwise, the walls were devoid of art or any decoration. The room left her with a cold impression.

When he came out, Josh was carrying a tray holding two glasses and a bottle of wine. He sat the tray on a table in front of the couch and poured wine into the glasses.

"Here's to us," he said, handing her one glass. "Another toast?"

"But I didn't want any wine." Angie paused a moment to

collect her thoughts. She felt pushed into making a toast with a beverage she didn't want. "Okay. To our budding friendship."

Josh raised his eyebrows. "Friendship?"

"Everything starts with friendship."

"Yes, true. Okay, to friendship." He gave her a dimpled smile.

They clinked glasses and Angie took one sip of her wine to appease Josh. It didn't take long after that for Josh to make his move, sliding closer on the couch. He put his arm around Angie and leaned in for a kiss, the scent of sandalwood overpowering her. This time it wasn't a soft, short kiss. He meant business.

"Oh, my wine," she said, holding her glass higher. "I'm spilling."

"It won't hurt. This is leather," Josh said. He swung his free arm to the table and placed his glass there, then took Angie's glass from her hand and put it beside his.

Again, he moved in for a kiss. When Angie squirmed a little, he placed his hand on the top of her upper arm, pressing her to the couch. Angie felt his hand press harder when she squirmed in response. She gave muffled protests as he persisted, finally having to push at him. His strong chest did not give way. Apparently, this was Josh's idea of a second date, but it certainly wasn't hers.

Angie pulled her face to the side when he came up for air. "Stop!"

The expression on Josh's face was one of surprise. "What?"

"Stop. I said stop and I meant it. I'm not doing this." Her mouth had formed a firm line of determination across her face.

Josh pulled himself away from her and sat back in the

couch, bringing his arm to his side. "Sorry. I just thought…" he said with a shrug.

"Well, think again. It's not happening."

"Okay," he said, throwing both his hands up in surrender. "Fine."

Angie looked carefully at his face, wondering what had possessed him to think she would comply. She didn't think she had given any indication she was easy.

"I think I should go," she said, standing. "Thank you for dinner, it was wonderful."

"Do you really have to go?"

"Yes. I have some time tomorrow before work to apply for a job. I need sleep." Angie walked with a determined stride to the front door. "I'll let myself out."

"I can walk you down," he offered.

"No, I'm safe. It's fine. Good night." She couldn't get away from him fast enough.

"Good night."

She walked to the elevator and pushed the fourth-floor button once inside. As she rode down, she thought about what had happened.

Rachel was sitting at the dining room table, slowly sipping her morning coffee. Joe walked in, looking at her suspiciously.

"You're up?"

It was six thirty, earlier than Rachel usually rose.

"Yes. I'm worried."

"About what?"

"Our daughter." She looked straight at her husband over the cup she was holding between her hands.

"Why are you worried now?"

"She didn't come home last night."

"I'll strangle that jerk if he thinks..." Joe's words choked off.

"I'm having similar thoughts, except mine are more graphic." Rachel took another sip of her coffee and then continued. "I went into her room because Precious was scratching at the door. I thought I'd tell her to feed the cat, except she wasn't in the bed. It was still perfectly made. So, I fed Precious. Then I saw her phone on the vanity. She didn't take her phone with her."

"That's unlike her. Maybe she forgot it?" Joe said. "You think she spent the night with Josh, don't you?"

Rachel rose from the chair, not answering the big question on her mind. "I'm going upstairs to speak with him."

"You're in a nightgown."

Rachel shot her husband an annoyed look. "Of course, I plan to change before I go."

"I can go with you."

"No, let me handle this. You'll get all male and protective." She knew how he could be regarding Angie.

"She's my daughter, of course I'll get protective. That's what dads do."

"There could be a good excuse," she said. "Not sure what that could be, but I'm going to ask."

Joe sighed audibly. "Okay, do what you want."

As soon as Rachel was dressed in the easiest thing she could find, jeans and a long- sleeved tee-shirt, she was out the door. She punched the button for the eighth floor, suddenly fuming, ready for bear. Her restraint was waning. One stupid comment and wham, she'd let him have it. Of course, she'd never hit anyone in her life. It was all hype running around in her brain.

After she arrived on the floor, she marched to unit 810, knocking loudly and ringing the doorbell. It took a minute for the door to open, given the time was early. Josh stuck his head out between the door and jamb.

"Oh, Rachel?" He looked bleary-eyed.

"Where is my daughter?"

"Your daughter? I don't know."

"Don't give me crap, Josh. Is Angie here?"

"No. Why would you think she's here?" he asked, opening the door fully. He looked like a man woken from sleep as he stood before her in a bathrobe, his hair askew.

"Because she's not home with us."

Josh shook his head. "That's not my problem. I'm sorry, Rachel, but I have no idea where Angie is."

"She's not with you?"

"No. She left here last night around ten."

"Did you walk her to our door?"

"No. She said she'd be fine. This is a secure building," he said with a shrug.

Rachel became silent, staring at Josh. "Then, where is she?"

"I don't know."

Rachel turned away in disbelief. *Where is my daughter*? She slowly walked back to the elevator, punching the fourth-floor button.

"Joe," she called as she walked into her unit. "She's not there."

Joe was in front of the stove stirring eggs in a small fry pan. Rufus was watching his every move. He turned around, pan in hand, spatula in the other, to face Rachel. "She wasn't at his place?"

"No."

Joe set the pan back on the stove. "Where could she be?"

Rachel just looked big eyed at her husband.

"Here, you sit and eat the eggs. I'm going to walk Rufus." Joe scraped the eggs onto a plate and set it on the small table.

He reached into the utensil drawer and brought out a fork, placing it beside the plate. "Sit. Eat."

Rachel did as she was told, sitting in the chair. She stared briefly at the eggs before picking up her fork.

"Here, Rufus. Walk time." Joe clipped the leash onto the collar. Rufus scampered toward the door. "Be back shortly."

Rachel chewed the eggs until they were almost liquid, staring into space. Her brain was fuzzy, as if she were looking at life through shredded cotton stretched from tree to tree during Halloween.

Joe returned quickly with Rufus, all but panting in his haste. "I have news about Angie," he said, unclipping the leash.

Rachel's head spun around. "What?"

"Our car is gone. She must have taken the car."

"The car? Why would she take the car? And where?"

"Beats me, but it's no longer in the parking space."

"She didn't come home last night..."

"Then she must have taken the car last night."

"For what? To get cigarettes? She doesn't smoke. What could be so important that she went out late at night?" Rachel looked blankly at her husband. "And without her phone?"

"Hey, you're asking the dad here. I was asleep."

"This just gets crazier. I'm still not sure Josh didn't have something to do with this."

Joe shrugged his shoulders. "No idea."

"Now what? Do we call the police?"

"I don't think so. She's an adult and could have driven – who knows where – and everything is fine."

"So, we wait?"

"We have to wait."

Rachel rolled her eyes and shook her head. Kids. Life didn't get any easier when they became adults.

FOURTEEN

AS SHE WAS ROOTING around in her purse for keys to the condo, she saw the car key attached to the ring. Angie immediately thought about taking a ride. To clear her head, think about what had happened. When the doors opened at the fourth floor, she pushed the close button and then the one for the lobby. She was going for a ride.

Angie turned right out of the parking lot and then left at the light, driving across the bridge to the mainland. She thought a drive near the river and park area would be relaxing, so that's where she directed the car. It was very peaceful this time of night. No one was on the back roads, and the only sound she heard was an owl through her open window. Just as she felt herself relax into her drive while weaving around the back roads near the river, life churned into a nightmare. At the only hairpin turn on the road, a semi-truck pulling a long trailer came flying at Angie's car. Not only was the driver going too fast to negotiate the turn, he wasn't even supposed to be on this road. And the pavement was damp, which in Florida meant the road was slick.

As the semi driver attempted to slow his speed and return to the correct lane, the trailer swung out in front of her. She slammed on her brakes to avoid it, but clipped the rear corner, which sent her hurling toward a light post. Angie watched in fascinated horror what happened next. It was just like in the movies, where everything is suddenly reduced to slow motion. Her car careened off the light post, bounced over some bushes, and crashed through the trees, finally diving nose first into a deep pit set about fifteen feet off the road.

The world suddenly became very still.

Minutes passed before Angie realized what had happened. She couldn't move, her body frozen like it was in the grip of a block of ice in the arctic or somewhere equally cold. She was helplessly stuck in the car as she turned her head around to understand where she was. Trees appeared to surround the vehicle, which probably concealed her presence from those driving past. Her parents' car was suspended over a pit, captured by broken down tree branches. Perhaps a sinkhole was a more appropriate term for where she found herself. The headlights illuminated a cavernous area that appeared to descend into the center of the earth. And then the headlights died.

Angie's mind began flitting around like one of the annoying mosquitos now entering the car. She noticed that her legs were securely encased in the crushed dashboard. While her arms were free and she could rotate her head around, fat chance that would release her from this trauma. Her parents' car was a twisted, mangled mess. They were going to be very upset.

Her saving grace was the seatbelt snuggly holding her in place. The airbag had malfunctioned, releasing a mere cotton ball sized puff. She imagined that the trucker had scooted away, probably oblivious to her situation.

Scary thoughts invaded her brain.

How long will I have to wait for help to arrive?

What if no one discovers me here?

What if no one ever finds me because I plunged farther down into this bottomless sinkhole?

The driver's side window had been in the down position prior to the accident, so air was traveling through. At least she could breathe easily even though she couldn't move anything below her head and shoulders.

I could die here.

"We haven't seen her since yesterday," Joe said to the police officer. "We know something's wrong because she hasn't contacted us."

When Angie didn't return to the apartment by six in the evening, they called the police to report her missing. They knew something was definitely wrong by this time. An officer came to their unit because they didn't have transportation.

"And she's in your car?" the officer asked as he wrote down the particulars.

"Yes, unless someone coincidentally stole our car at the same time," Rachel said.

"Unlikely," he said.

"I know. Here is the license number and description of our car." She handed the second officer a slip of paper she had prepared with the vehicle's information written on it.

"Does she know the area?" he asked.

"She was born in this area, so yes, she knows her way around," Joe said.

"Is she suicidal?"

"Mercy, no," Rachel said. "She's quite sane. Someone has kidnapped her or something awful has happened. She isn't going to harm herself. But you should talk to Josh Brigham. He lives in 810. He's the last one to see her."

"I'll do that. Anyone else you know of who might have seen her?

"No."

"One of you said you had a picture?" The man looked back and forth at both of them.

"Yes, here," Joe said, reaching beside himself for the picture on the table. "This is recent."

"Okay, we'll get this information out immediately. Having the car's information will help a lot and, of course, the picture." The officer stood, adjusting the holster near his leg. "I'll let you know as things occur."

"Thank you, officer," Joe said.

"Yes, thank you. Anything else you need, just let us know," Rachel said.

"Take care, folks." Both men left the condo.

Joe and Rachel stood near the door, numbly staring at each other. No words were needed. They knew each other's thoughts after so many years of marriage.

News leaked out to the residents about Angie's disappearance. It began as people noticed Rachel and Joe being around, yet their car was gone. One thing led to another and the word was out.

"I'm so sorry," was the first thing Ruby said after she entered the office. Ethel was with her, wearing a coverup over her bathing suit, to Rachel's relief. "Any news yet?"

"No, not a word." The expression Rachel wore was clearly one of grief.

"Sheesh. How can someone vanish?" Ethel said through her nose, hands on her hips.

"I don't know." Rachel's chest heaved with a sigh. "I keep praying, 'God protect my baby.'"

The old lady looked kindly at her. "Well, I'll leave you. I just wanted to ask if you knew anything."

"Not yet."

"I'll pray for her, too," Ethel said, turning to leave.

Ruby turned around from the door just before she left. "I almost forgot to tell you something."

"What's that?"

"I think I know who the man is in the topcoat and hat."

"Really? You know our mystery man?"

"Yeah. I think it's my ex-husband, well, one of them anyway. Bob Mason is his name."

"Your ex? How about that." Rachel sat back, amused and confused.

"Yeah. Don't know why he'd be snooping around, but that's who it is."

"Thanks Ruby."

FIFTEEN

ANGIE DECIDED TO THINK POSITIVE, given she was frozen into position and couldn't help herself. How will she occupy her time? She hadn't expected some idiot trucker to be driving too fast on damp pavement and on a road he wasn't even supposed to be on in the first place. So, she decided to put a positive spin on her situation. The positive view was that she always fastened her seatbelt and this event had been no different. That seatbelt had saved her life. The car landed right side up, although pitched forward. Hanging upside down would have made an awful situation even worse. Therefore, life could have been truly awful instead of just a little.

Angie hoped someone driving by would see her before she spent another night trapped in the car. While this wasn't a busy road, cars were periodically traveling by. She could see them between the trees, but could they see her? It only took one to see her in the pit. Just one, and she would be freed. But then, she really didn't know how visible her car was from the road, if at all. But that wasn't a positive thought.

As the day wore on, the situation grew increasingly boring, and Angie grew hungrier with each passing hour. She hadn't eaten since dinner with Josh. Now it appeared that any sort of food was a fanciful thought at best until she was rescued. Angie was also hot. It was hazy outside and humid, typical Florida weather for this time of year. And she was very thirsty. She scanned the interior of the car for a bottle of water. She saw a bottle on the passenger side floor, but reaching it was a problem. Then she noticed an umbrella caught between the top half of the passenger seat and the lower portion. Angie grabbed it with her right hand and wiggled the end toward the bottle. She managed to drag it closer to her.

Now she had to stretch to reach it. Laying over on her right side, Angie extended her arm down to reach the bottle. Thank goodness for her years practicing yoga at the ashrams. Fingertips touched the plastic cap, then the neck, and finally she was able to curl two fingers around the neck of the bottle. Success!

Using the steering wheel, she pulled herself upright again with her left arm. Angie unscrewed the cap and lifted the bottle to her lips, enjoying the liquid refreshment, taking care not to drink all the water in case she needed it later.

As the evening wore on, she became sleepy, especially when it became dark. It was still humid, but less so. She wondered if she could sleep? But what else did she have to do? She couldn't watch TV or chat on the phone. And where *was* her phone? She didn't even know where her purse was at the moment. Angie decided that she might as well sleep until help came to rescue her. She was thinking positive! Help was coming! And that's when the thunderstorm began. Soon the rain was briskly beating into the car through the open window while thunder boomed above, rattling the car and her nerves. As she watched a streak of lightning dance across the sky, she felt the vehicle jerk down about a foot. Angie shrieked and froze in position as the rain continued to saturate half her torso. She dared not move for fear the car would plunge further into the sinkhole.

"God help me!" she cried out.

As quickly as the storm came, the thunder stopped, the skies cleared, and the lightning was no more. Peace replaced the terrifying moments. And the humidity was gone. Angie closed her eyes and attempted sleep. But several times during the night, she woke up when she heard wildlife rustling around in the bushes. And then there was a noisy owl hooting nearby for all he was worth. Adding to her distractions and discomfort was the soggy feeling of the seat underneath and her clothes stuck to half her body.

"Please, God, help me. Send someone to find me here. I'm a nice girl. I don't steal, swear, cheat, and I'm not promiscuous. Help me, God." Tears began to track down her cheeks,

Things really are bad when I start to plead with God. She knew better than to bargain. That was not the way to get what she needed. But prayer was. She had been raised as a Christian, attended Sunday school, went to church, spent weeks in vacation Bible school, and summer camp, all of it. But as an adult, she had strayed toward eastern religions.

She supposed she was looking for answers or something exciting, a new adventure. Otherwise, she really didn't know what she had been looking for back then or why she sought answers from other religions when the one she had always comforted her and fulfilled her needs.

Her mother, who hadn't really gone to church much when Angie was a little girl, was now attending regularly, reading the Bible, and going to Bible study. She had changed a lot, while her dad had always been religious and continued to be. Perhaps it was time to return to her roots? Her parents attended services every Sunday. She could go with them to church. Maybe it was time. *I just have to get out of this sinkhole.*

Joe and Rachel sat side by side on the couch the next morning. They clasped hands while Joe led them in prayer. Of course, the prayer was asking for their daughter to be brought home safely. Rachel's tears ran steadily down her cheeks, one chasing the other, as Joe spoke the words aloud.

"Amen," they said together at the end of the prayer.

"It's going to be okay," Joe said to Rachel. "Don't worry, God's got this."

Rachel nodded her head and tried to smile. "Yes, of course. I'm going into the office. It will keep me busy."

"Good idea."

"We have dinner in the crockpot."

"Sounds like a plan." Joe patted his wife's shoulder and leaned in to kiss her cheek. She gave him a halfhearted smile and stood to leave for her office.

Josh was the first person to enter Rachel's office, dressed as always in black. He nodded at her, hesitating to speak.

"Yes, Josh, what is it?" Rachel wasn't standing on ceremony today. She was nursing hurt.

"I just wanted to know if you'd heard anything?"

"No, nothing so far," she said, sitting back in her chair. "The police are on the lookout for the car. They feel if they can find the car, it will lead them to Angie."

"I'm very sorry."

Rachel looked up at the young man, so tall and handsome. "You were the last one to see her."

"I know."

"I still think you are more involved in this than you're saying."

"No, I am not. I don't know any more than you. And that's exactly what I told the police."

Rachel fixed her gaze on Josh's face. She didn't believe him. Her daughter disappeared after being with him. No phone call, no text. Something wasn't right about this situation. And Josh was involved, as far as she was concerned.

"Whatever, Josh."

"I'm very sorry," he said, and walked out of the office.

Rachel ground her teeth in frustration. Her precious daughter, missing. Tears sprang to her eyes. They hadn't always gotten along. There was that period of time when she was a teenager seeking her identity, wanting to be independent. They had clashed many times, but during this season in life, they were actually doing quite well. Now, this. She shook her head, wiped her tears with her fingers and pressed on with paperwork to keep herself busy.

Rachel heard a soft tap at the door, then Penelope walked in. Practically no one knocked before entering, probably because they thought she could see them approach through the glass walls.

"Hello, Penelope."

"Yes, hello." The old lady looked at her, then sighed. "I hate to complain. You know I don't do that often, but sometimes one just has to tell the truth."

"What's the matter?"

"That new neighbor on my floor. I think she belongs in the loony bin."

"Who are you talking about?" So many of the residents displayed idiosyncrasies, it was hard to know who she was speaking about.

"Gladys Porter. The one with the wild hair. You know, the one that looks like Phyllis Diller."

"Oh, yes, she does, doesn't she?" Gladys was fairly new to

the condo. To Rachel's knowledge, she was quiet and kept to herself. But if the old lady was misbehaving, Penelope could be counted on to report the behavior. "So, what is she doing?"

"Around eight o'clock every other morning, Gladys dons her tennis shoes and shorts and goes for a run," Penelope said.

"What's wrong with that?"

"Well, besides the fact that she has no business running like she thinks she's sixteen, Gladys stops in front of my unit and crows like a rooster."

Rachel had to stifle a chuckle. "Like a rooster? Is she trying to wake you up?"

"I don't know what she's doing. I just think it's a little insane to crow at someone's door, don't you?" Penelope clutched her pink cardigan closer to her body.

Rachel had to agree, this was odd behavior. "Yes, it's a bit strange. Why don't you ask her why she's doing the crowing?"

"Oh, I couldn't do that. No." Penelope shook her head. "That's your job."

Rachel didn't agree. The crowing wasn't bothering anyone but Penelope. But she had to placate the woman. "I will talk with her the next time I see her, okay?"

"Yes. That's all I'm asking." The old lady turned to the door. "Thank you, dear."

After Penelope had left, Rachel let out a hoot. This was a new one, crowing. Maybe the woman was a bit eccentric, but she appeared harmless. And she fit right in with the other quirky residents.

"I hope I can sleep," Rachel said to her husband in between brushing her teeth and spitting out froth.

"I know the feeling," he said. "I'm wondering the same thing. This has gone on far too long not to be something serious. Something is awfully wrong."

"Yes." Her eyes looked into the mirror. Her face was drawn. She looked tired. "We just don't know what it is."

They both crawled into bed quietly. Rufus joined them, lying across the foot of the bed, his body almost spanning the width. Benny crept over to lie between Joe and Rachel. Precious was sequestered in the other bedroom awaiting her mistress's return.

After tossing around a little, Rachel was able to fall asleep. No hot flashes or cold chills, either. She slept very well until five o'clock when she woke with a start.

"Joe!" she called out, punching him in the back with her fist to wake him. "I know where she is!" Rachel continued by shaking him awake until he rolled onto his back.

Joe squinted at his wife. "What? What's wrong now?" He had been sound asleep and was groggy, not understanding his wife's excitedness.

Rachel shook his arm. "Joe, I know where Angie is."

"Where?"

"In a ditch. I saw her in my dream." Rachel was known to have prophetic dreams. She'd had them since being a teenager. When Eneida was murdered, Rachel had dreamt about it before it happened. And now this.

"Where's the ditch? I can go there now."

"In what car? I don't know exactly where it is, but I can describe it."

"Let's call Detective France, he'll know what to do," Joe said, rolling out of bed. "He'll also believe you."

"Yes, that's important," Rachel said, realizing not all law enforcement personnel were as open minded as France.

Joe hastily walked to the living room, taking hold of the

landline receiver. He wanted the number and location to show on their computers when he called dispatch.

"Yes, Detective France," he was saying as Rachel came into the room. "I know it's early, but she's been missing, and we need him to come here so we can give him some information."

Rachel sat in a chair while her husband handled the dispatch operator.

"Yeah, I know, but he'll know us, so just call him, would you, please?" Joe shook his head as he looked at his wife. "Right, yes. Thank you very much."

"What happened?"

"She said she would call him, and he will contact us," Joe said, sitting beside Rachel.

"How long?"

"She didn't say."

"Hmm. If we had a car, we could go look ourselves."

"Yeah, well, the car is with Angie."

"So it is. You need to rent us a car, and I'll make some coffee. We can't go back to sleep now," she said, rising. "Call an agency."

"The last time you did this, we walked into a murder at 810." Joe gave his wife a knowing expression.

"I know. I'm hoping the dream is just a clue and not a prelude to tragedy." Rachel walked to the kitchen to make coffee.

A couple hours passed before the phone rang. Joe grabbed the phone after one ring.

"Hello?"

"Detective France here. Joe?"

"Yes, it is."

"They said you had news about your missing daughter."

"Yes, Rachel had one of her dreams. She thought you would take her seriously, so we wanted to speak to you."

"Of course. What did she dream?"

"I'll let you talk to Rachel," he said, motioning for her to come take the phone.

"Detective France? It's Rachel," she said. "I knew you would understand."

"Yes, ma'am. What happened in the dream?"

"I saw a car hit a light post and fly into the air. It landed on top of trees and fell into a sinkhole. It was a bit exaggerated, but the car did come to rest in a pit or sinkhole, something like that."

"I see. What else? Where is the sinkhole?"

"I'm not sure, but I think it's near water and there are lots of trees around. The car could be hidden, it looked to me." Explaining dreams to someone was difficult for Rachel.

"Is Angie in the car?"

"I didn't see that. All I saw was the car with the frontend bent down into a big ditch or sinkhole."

"Okay, I'll have patrol look around the river. Since you live near the river, that's a likely start."

"Thank you so much, Detective France," she said before hanging up.

SIXTEEN

ANGIE FELT WEAK. She had drunk all the water available, trying to stretch it as far as possible. Not having eaten for so long, she felt shaky and confused. All she could do was lie back on the seat and wait. And wait. That's all she had been doing for what seemed like days, even though it had not been that long. She endured mosquitos attacking like dive bombers and been terrified a few times by animal noises during the night. Her worst fear was a gator coming along and sliding through the window. But she wasn't sure they were in this area. She had never heard of a gator attack before, but then, she wasn't an avid reader of the newspaper. And she hadn't lived in the area for many years.

In the quiet of the setting, she heard someone singing. It was faint, but loud enough to recognize the tune. An oldy but a goody; she knew the words well enough to sing along. Angie tried to muster enough strength to call for help. Previous attempts had been fruitless.

"Help!" she croaked out in a raspy voice. She waited a few seconds, but the singer kept on singing. She tried twice more. Then she no longer could hear the singer.

Feeling dejected, Angie began to cry. Her one hope for rescue, and it sang off into the distance. After several minutes of feeling sorry for herself, Angie heard something stirring in the brush.

"Oh, no, what now?" She envisioned a bear approaching. Or maybe a snake slithering through the leaves. Weren't they able climb? Maybe climb into the car? She cried out in frustration.

"Miss? You okay?"

A young boy stood just above her at the edge of the sinkhole. He looked to be about twelve. He was peering down at her, gripping a branch in front of him.

"Help me…Help."

"I'll get some help, miss."

The boy disappeared as quickly as he had appeared. Angie's eyes grew wide as her heart danced in her chest.

Is help coming?

Joe opened the door to Rachel's office halfway, sticking his head inside.

"Get your purse. They found her."

Rachel grabbed her purse, clicked off the lights and was out the door in seconds. Joe was holding the door open to the outside as a patrol car approached the curb. An officer exited and opened the back door for them.

"Get inside, folks. I can get you to the hospital faster."

Rachel slid across the seat and Joe sat next to her.

"What happened?" Rachel asked.

"She's in the Halifax Hospital," Joe said. "They found the car near the river in a sinkhole, like you saw in the dream. She's okay."

"So, how did she end up there?" Rachel demanded answers after having none for so long.

"Ma'am," the officer said from the front seat, "your daughter's going to be all right. Somehow, she ended up stuck in a sinkhole. A kid found her and flagged us down when we were searching for her in that area. It's a good thing, too. She was off the road enough and down in the sinkhole, so we might not have seen her just from driving by because of the trees."

"Thank you, God," Rachel said, placing her hands in a prayer position. "How bad is she hurt?"

"I wasn't there, so I don't know. I don't think bad." He crossed traffic at an intersection by flashing his emergency lights and letting his siren sound briefly.

"Okay, okay. It's all going to be fine," she said aloud to comfort herself. "Everything is good. She's alive, thank God, she's alive."

After a short drive, the officer pulled the patrol car over to the entrance of the Emergency Room. Joe and Rachel sped through the entrance to the admitting desk. "Angie Barnes," Rachel said to the woman behind the counter with her hair drawn back into a bun. "She was brought in; we're her parents."

"Please be seated. I'll check on her."

The woman spoke to someone on the phone and then motioned Joe and Rachel to come back to the counter.

"She is assigned to room 312 and will be taken there very soon. You can go up there and wait for her if you want," the woman said.

"Yes, we want to," Rachel said.

They turned away from the counter and walked from the ER into the main portion of the hospital. They found an elevator and rode in silence to the third floor. When the elevator doors opened, they quickly found the room and sat down, waiting for their daughter, neither speaking.

It wasn't long before Angie was brought into the room on

a stretcher. Her face was pale and marked by what looked like many red bug bites, as were her arms. Otherwise, they couldn't see any injury.

"Angie!" they both cried and jumped up at the sight of their daughter.

"Mom, Dad," she said sleepily.

The aides placed her in the bed, adjusting the level of the portion against her back, and fussing with the pillow. The metal apparatus holding fluids that were attached to her wrist by tubes was wheeled close to the bed. Once the staff left, they began to talk.

"How are you? What's wrong?" Now standing beside the bed, Rachel asked the questions in the most worried voice she had ever used as a mother.

"I'm dehydrated and I haven't eaten in days, so they're trying to rehydrate and nourish me," she said slowly, cupping the top of the sheet in both hands. "I also have a ton of mosquito bites, and my legs are very bruised. I also have some lacerations, but other than that, I'm okay."

"I'm speechless," Rachel said. "I thought you could be dead, or someone kidnapped you."

Joe looked seriously at her from across the bed. "Yeah, awful thoughts ran through my mind, too. But you're alive and okay. I'm so relieved. We're so relieved."

Rachel let out a long sigh of relief and closed her eyes. "Thank God you're all right."

"We've been praying for you. Our church has been praying, too," Joe said. "Our prayers have been answered." Tears formed in his eyes and he looked down.

"Oh, Daddy." Angie smiled at her father and then her mother. "You can relax now. I'll probably go home tomorrow. But I do have some bad news."

"What's that?" Joe asked.

"Your car is totaled. You need to get a new car."

"That could be good news," Rachel said with a grin.

"Yeah, I guess that's to be expected," Joe said, rubbing the top of his head. "Tell us about the accident."

They pulled the two available chairs in the room closer to the bed as Angie began to speak.

"Well, you know I went out to eat with Josh. When we got back home, we went upstairs to his place. He wanted me to meet his father," she said, deciding to leave out the advance Josh put on her. "Later, I rode in the elevator to go home and decided to go for a ride instead. To just think. It never crossed my mind you'd care if I used the car. Better than walking around late at night, right? Well, so I thought."

She rolled her eyes and took a breath before she continued. "I drove for a while near the river until this truck driver came flying around a curve in the road. The pavement was damp, he skidded, and the trailer swung out at me. I braked, clipped the trailer, bounced into a light pole, and careened into a sink hole. Could only happen to me. Probably the only sinkhole near the river, so I found it."

"What happened with the trucker? Didn't he help you?" Rachel asked.

"I don't know what happened to him. He probably didn't know I landed in a sinkhole," Angie said. "I never saw him again."

"And you couldn't get out?" Joe asked.

"No, the dash was crushed all around my legs; I couldn't move. That's where all the bruises came from."

"What did you do while you were waiting?" Rachel asked.

"Absolutely nothing. I was bored silly. And starving. There wasn't anything to eat. I was lucky I found a bottle of water that was in front of the passenger seat. Otherwise, I don't know how I would have survived without water." Angie moved her head around to gain more comfort.

"And some kid found you?" Joe asked. "That's what I was told."

"Yes. I heard him singing, so I called for help. He came over and saw me, then went to get the police. Bless that little guy's heart. Oh, and then it got crazy when the police came. They had to pull the car out in order to get to me. They were afraid the walls of the sinkhole would collapse and pull the car inside or other people." Her eyes began to sparkle, indicating she was feeling emotional. "But they gave me water while that was happening. Then they had to use the jaws of life to free me from the car. It was amazing."

"What a story…You had an angel protecting you," Rachel said.

"I sure did." Angie smiled broadly, causing her parents' hearts to swell with love.

The next day Joe and Rachel set out to buy a new car. He wanted an SUV, but Rachel didn't think she could see over the steering wheel.

"Something smaller. Easy to park," she suggested.

They went to several dealerships, finally ending at Kia.

"I always thought the Soul was so cute," Rachel said, pointing toward a line of Souls in a variety of colors parked nearby.

The salesman escorted them to the line of cars. Immediately, Rachel fell in love with a white one. "That one, Joe. I like that one."

The couple did a test drive to make sure Rachel was comfortable in the vehicle and Joe thought it practical. The car was great on mileage and had a good consumer report. Rachel looked up at Joe with big eyes. He knew the look. The look said, buy it. And so, they did.

SEVENTEEN

WHEN ANGIE WALKED into the diner, a burst of applause greeted her.

"Yay, Angie!" people called out.

She felt a little embarrassed over the attention and didn't feel she deserved any praise for surviving an accident. She waved the attention away and entered the kitchen.

"Angie! We were worried about you," Brian said. "Your mother told us they didn't know where you were."

"Yeah, I was hiding out in the bushes with the mosquitoes," she joked. "But I'm back."

"Your admirer has been asking about you," Sara said. "I've been waiting on him."

"Oh, not good news," Angie said, wrapping the apron around her waist over her pink uniform. "Why can't he go away?"

"I told him," Brian said.

"Apparently he didn't listen."

Angie stepped into the dining area to begin setting up tables for the next shift. It wasn't long before James walked in. As soon as he saw her, his face lit up. A broad smile crossed his face as he made his way to a private booth in Angie's section.

"Hello, James," Angie said, pulling out her tablet and pen. "What do you want today?"

His hand shot out, clasping her wrist. "I'm so happy to see you safe."

"Ah, a little accident can't keep me down," she said, trying to make light conversation. "Your order?"

"You're not busy, why the rush?"

"I have other things to do besides wait on customers. Your order?"

Reluctantly, James gave his order.

"Here we go again," she said as she clipped the paper on the metal holder. "Ugh."

Angie brought a can of soda to the table for James, dropping a straw accidentally on the floor. James reached for her hand before she could retrieve the straw. "No worry. Leave it."

"James," she started, "I know Brian talked to you about leaving me alone. This is not leaving me alone."

"I don't want to leave you alone. I'm in love with you," he said, looking into her eyes. "And you could love me, too, if you'd just give us a chance."

"I don't think so. You're much older than me, so I'm not interested."

"But you could be. You have to give our love a chance," he said, still holding her hand.

"James, I don't want to. Understand? I do not want to give what you call love any chance or attention, nada, zippo, no." Angie pulled her hand back and walked away. She hid out in the kitchen until the order came up.

"Sara, take this to James. I'm done." Angie handed the plate to the other woman. "You can have the tip."

Sara walked away with a smile on her face and the plate

in her hand over to where James was seated. He looked disappointed to see Sara instead of Angie. His eyes skipped past Sara to where Angie stood shaking her head at James. She even mouthed the word no to get her point across. James ate quickly and left.

The rest of her time at the diner wasn't quite as eventful. That is, until a skinny delivery boy entered with a bouquet of flowers. For Angie, of course. No one had to be a nuclear scientist to know whose name was on the attached card.

"I'm so glad you agreed to meet me," Josh said as he sat across the table from Angie. "I owe you an apology for my behavior. And I wanted to see how you are after your accident."

"I'm okay. I still have bruises on my legs, but they'll heal," she said. When he texted her, she hesitated to respond, but decided to give him another chance. What could it hurt? There wasn't a parade of guys lined up to ask her out.

"You still have bites on your chin."

"I do. But they will heal as well."

"You have such a positive attitude. I don't know if I would be so positive if I were in your shoes," he said, taking a sip from the coffee mug.

"How can I be negative? I survived. I lived through what could have been a crippling accident," she said, raising her shoulders and smiling. "God is good."

"You believe in God?" he asked with a slight frown.

"Yes, I do. Don't you?"

"I'm not as sure as you."

"Hmm, well, He exists," she said. "I know."

"I'd like to make up for being so pushy with you. What can I do?" he asked, changing the subject. "I'm not usually that way."

Angie doubted that was true. "I don't know…Take me

back to that restaurant and we can begin again? Like nothing happened."

"I like that idea."

"Me, too."

"So, you've gone back to work?" he asked, changing the subject.

"Yes. Nothing has changed there," she said, sipping her latte.

"What about that guy who's been bothering you?"

"Nothing has changed there, either. He is relentless, despite Brian talking to him," she said, shaking her head. "And to top it all off, he had flowers delivered to the diner for my return. How embarrassing."

Josh's jaw tightened. "I don't understand why this old guy can't take a hint. And flowers? Something has to be done about him."

"I know, except he isn't taking no for an answer. I don't know what to do," she said, brushing the hair away from her face that was blocking the coffee cup.

"I do."

"Honey, I was so scared for you," LuAnn said, drumming her long nails on the side of her mug. "I can't imagine what you were going through."

"It must have been awful," Olivia said, all wide eyed and breathless. "I would have taken to the bed for sure if any of my babies were missing."

"It was awful. I saw myself losing my child, my only child, and possibly never finding her body to know what happened," Rachel said, batting her lashes to keep back the tears.

"Precious girl," Olivia said, placing a comforting hand over Rachel's wrist.

"Thank goodness that is over. Now we can return to our normal dramas," LuAnn said, lifting her mug to her rosy lips.

"So, what is your current drama?" Rachel asked. "I feel I've been out of touch for a while. Isn't your gig going well?"

"Oh my, yes, it's terrific, no issues there."

"So, what's your issue?" Olivia asked, patting the sides of her wig. She had a new one, very poufy and straighter than what she usually wore.

"Derks. What else could it be?" LuAnn took a sip of her drink.

"What's wrong with him? I thought he was the perfect man in every way," Rachel asked.

"He really is, honey, he's just noncommittal," LuAnn drawled, placing the mug on the table. "He doesn't want to see other women, just me. He doesn't want a future without me. He doesn't want to perform with anyone else but me."

"My hearing is perfect," Rachel said. "Nowhere in those sentences did I hear a negative."

"Oh, no, none of that is negative. He just doesn't want to talk about marriage. That's a negative." LuAnn took both of her hands to hoist the top of her blue shirt that had crept down over her bosomy chest so she could conceal some of her ample cleavage that was peeking out.

"There are advantages to being single," Olivia said. "I've been single a long time since my husband died. The longer it goes, the more I enjoy my independence."

LuAnn turned her full gaze on Olivia. "That's you, not me. I want a husband."

"Well, if you want my opinion, I prefer marriage," Rachel said. "I can't imagine life without Joe. He has been my rock through many issues. He helped me when I discovered I had diabetes, to name a large issue we struggled through. And recently, thinking we'd lost our little girl."

"Honey, Joe is a keeper, no doubt there. I thought Derks was, too," LuAnn said, sticking her full lips out in a pout.

"LuAnn, you've only been seeing each other for, what, a few months?" Olivia said. "Give the guy a break. Give him more time. He'll probably come around after you've been together a year."

LuAnn looked aghast at that idea. "*A year?* I don't want to waste a year of my life if this isn't going anywhere."

"I think it's going somewhere, LuAnn," Rachel said. "He isn't interested in a personal or professional life without you, according to what you just said. So, give him time. Marriage is a big step. Cut the guy some slack, okay?'

LuAnn looked at her friend, carefully weighing what she said. "Okay. I'll try to be patient."

"Good girl," Rachel said.

"Cheers to that," Olivia said, raising her glass.

EIGHTEEN

ANGIE'S FATHER was relaxing on the balcony, enjoying a peaceful evening. They had finished eating dinner. Her mother was reading in the bedroom and she was watching TV in the living room. Her parents had just closed on their investment, so her dad was feeling inspired to begin work at the house. His maintenance duties would have to blend with his new job of fixing up the Victorian. Tonight, he was enjoying reading the newspaper. Life had swung back to normal after she had been found in the sinkhole.

"Holy cow," Joe said aloud, taking a second read of the first few sentences in an article, and then continuing through to the end. He got up from the chair and came inside, tossing the paper at Angie. "Read that first article. That's your diner."

Angie opened the newspaper to the heading *Diner Patron Attacked.* "Holy cow, someone was attacked at my diner!"

Rachel came out of the bedroom, dressed in a pale pink nightie and holding a book. "What happened?"

"You won't believe this!" Angie said, obviously upset. She read a portion of the article aloud. "'A man known to frequent Brian's Burgers was brutally attacked in the parking lot after his meal. Employees said he was known to them as James.' Mom! I know him!"

"How do you know him?" Joe asked.

"He's a regular. I wait on him all the time. He kinda likes me. A little too much, actually. Remember, I told you about him?" Angie said, looking back and forth between her parents. "And he was attacked."

"It says there were no witnesses," Joe said.

"Yeah, another customer found him lying on the ground and called police." Angie closed the paper. "They don't know if he'll recover."

She felt bad for James. She also had some suspicions about the attacker. Josh had mentioned 'something needing to be done' about James. Could he have carried out his insinuation that he knew how to take care of things? Was he that kind of man?

Angie went into her bedroom, excusing herself from her parents. She clicked on her laptop and Googled Josh's name. Nothing showed up locally about him. It took some time to scan county records in a few states that he had mentioned having business. She gave up on that after having no success. Nevada was the most likely place to search. Finally, she located an arrest for him in that state. The mugshot accompanying the report made it clear she had the right person. The report stated the arrest happened eighteen months ago and was for aggravated battery. A man was seriously beaten in a parking lot at a gambling casino. That was a familiar scenario. Assaulting a man in a parking lot? Chasing more information, Angie found records indicating Josh had beaten the charge due to a technicality during the arrest. In her mind that meant he did the deed but got away with it due to sloppy police work.

Angie looked up from the laptop. *Who is Josh Brigham?*

. . .

Rachel was in her office sorting through applications for residency. Ruby walked in, smiling. She was wearing a green dress that was very becoming. The color accentuated her blazing red hair and bright red lipstick. Rachel wasn't sure she had ever seen Ruby in a dress.

"I have someone I want you to meet," Ruby said, reaching out the door to pull in a tall man with white hair and dressed in a suit. "Rachel, this is Bob Mason. My ex-husband."

Rachel immediately stood to greet the man, extending her hand toward him.

"I'm delighted to meet you, Bob."

"It's my pleasure to meet you, young lady," he said warmly. "The women in Florida are such beauties."

Rachel chuckled. "Oh, you are quite the charmer, huh?"

"If so, only because you bring it out," Bob said through very white teeth.

"I'm sorry, I only have the one chair," she said, pointing at it, "but please stay and chat."

Ruby took the chair and Bob stood beside her.

"Are you in town for long?"

Bob looked down at Ruby. "That depends on her."

"He can stay as long as he wants," Ruby said. "We have a lot of catching up to do."

"I would think so," Rachel said, sitting again in her chair. "But how did you come to be here?"

Bob rolled his head around as if he were loosening his neck. "I started missing Ruby, so I hired a private detective to find her. The first time I came here, I couldn't get in the door."

"Yes, I know. I received a report of a man dressed oddly for Florida attempting to gain entry."

"Ha! That was me. I tried again, but no luck. I kept trying, but I never timed it right to follow someone in," he said with a little sigh. "Finally, I gave up and contacted Ruby."

"Why didn't you do that in the first place?" Rachel asked.

"I wanted to just show up at her door, be a big surprise. Tada, here I am!" He patted the shoulder he had his hand resting on.

"He was a surprise, all right," Ruby said, smiling up at the man and touching his hand at her shoulder. "We haven't seen each other since we were in our fifties."

"That long? Well, I guess you've both changed considerably since then," Rachel said, grinning at the couple.

"Oh, Ruby's still my shining star," Bob said. "She's hardly changed at all."

Rachel and Ruby both knew that wasn't true, but the old woman still beamed over the compliment.

"How long were you married?"

"About five years, right?" Ruby said, looking up at Bob.

"Yes, five years. Five rowdy years."

Ruby laughed. "Rowdy is the word. I wasn't ready to settle down. He was a gambler back then. We just hit it at the wrong time."

"You weren't ready to settle down in your fifties?" Rachel asked.

"Nah, not me," she said, waving her hand in response. "And he was my fourth husband."

"Fourth?"

"Oh, yeah," she said, nodding. "I had two others after that."

"Ruby! You crazy woman!" Rachel couldn't believe what she was hearing. She had never known anyone to have six marriages.

"But this guy was the best of them," Ruby said, reaching up to take his arm in her hand. "He spoiled me rotten."

"You deserved every bit," he said, patting her hand.

"Well, I can see you two are an item to watch."

Rachel was very pleased.

NINETEEN

JOSH PULLED the chair out for Angie and scooted her to the table. They were seated at the exact table in the same restaurant as before. Again, they were given preferential treatment when they arrived. The server brought two menus and left after taking their drink order.

"What are you in the mood for?" Josh asked as he scanned the menu.

"Oysters? That sounds good to me."

"Ugh, squishy and slimy." Josh scowled.

"Not when fried."

"I still don't like them."

"Hmm, your loss. They're delicious." Angie didn't care about his preferences. She loved oysters.

The server brought Angie a glass of iced tea and Josh a martini.

"The lady will have the fried oysters," Josh said. "Slaw?" he asked of her.

"Yes, please, slaw with the fries."

"I'll have the grouper, baked potato and slaw."

"Very good," the server said and left again.

"Let's try another toast," Josh said, raising his glass. "To a wonderful evening with a beautiful woman."

Angie raised her glass and clinked against his. "Thank you." She was wearing a blue dress that set off the color of her blue eyes. Pearl earrings pierced her ears, peeking out from under her flowing hair, and a matching single strand necklace graced her neck. Her mother had given her the set for Christmas one year because she felt every woman should have pearls.

She turned her head to look at the sea rolling in to shore. It was breathtaking and powerful. The majesty of mother nature, the power and beauty. She turned back and studied Josh's face. He seemed less relaxed tonight.

"How long are you in town for?" she asked

"Not sure. So far Dad doesn't need me to go anywhere. Everything is calm." After he said the words, he quickly added a smile, like it was an afterthought.

"Have you ever been to Diablo, Nevada?" That was the town where Angie now knew he had assaulted that man.

Josh looked surprised to hear the name, but quickly recovered. "Diablo? Not that I recall. Why?"

"I have a friend there and she invited me to visit her," she said, prepared with a fib. "I wondered what it was like."

"I wouldn't know, but I've been in Nevada numerous times. It's hot and dry. I prefer the weather here." He stirred the olive skewered on the pic in his glass. "Don't go in the summer. Brutally hot."

"Umm, I imagine."

"Have you been looking for another job?" he said, steering her away from Nevada.

"I had the chance one day to interview for two, but then I had that accident, so I didn't follow up," she said, sliding her hair behind her ear. "I need to get serious about job hunting."

"Yes, or you'll be at that diner forever."

The server brought their food to the table. The oysters looked beautifully cooked, but the eyes on Josh's grouper staring out from the plate repulsed Angie. She never could eat anything that looked back at her from the plate.

"Excuse me," she said, leaning a dessert menu on the lantern in the center of the table, blocking the view of Josh's plate. "I can't look at the eyes of that fish. It's gross."

"Are you kidding?"

"No, I'm definitely not kidding."

Josh gave her a disgusted look and shook his head. "Whatever. Sometimes I eat the eyeballs."

"Now you're kidding. I hope."

"Yeah, I'm kidding." Josh chuckled at her aghast expression.

Angie looked at her oysters, wondering if she could eat them after that remark. Taking a deep breath, she cut one in half and dipped that portion into tartar sauce, then popped it into her mouth. It was perfectly cooked, so she relaxed into eating her dinner, carefully avoiding looking at Josh as he fed fish into his mouth.

"Do you want dessert?" he asked after finishing his meal.

"No, I try to avoid sweets."

"Me, too. Coffee?"

"Sure. That would be nice."

The server took their plates and returned with coffee and a shot of brandy for Josh. Angie added some cream to her cup and contentedly sipped her coffee.

"Josh…do you remember me mentioning that man that was annoying me at work?" Angie carefully trained her eyes on Josh's face.

"Yes," he said, looking directly at her.

"I saw in the newspaper that he was attacked in the parking lot where I work."

"Really?"

"Yes, he was beaten. Brutally so, the article said." Her eyes never left his face.

"That's too bad." His tone did not suggest sympathy. He poured his brandy into the coffee.

"Yes, it really is."

"Hey, but he sort of deserved it, right?" Josh half smiled at her. "Look how he treated you."

Angie tilted her head back, so she was looking down her nose at Josh. "He was never unkind, just a pest. Do you really think a pest deserves to be brutally beaten?"

Josh was silent, apparently realizing he'd made a bad move. "Well, maybe not, but he deserved punishment, didn't he?"

"Punishment? A brutal beating? That's excessive punishment if you ask me." Angie was really wondering about her date. No empathy, no compassion. What kind of man was he?

"Maybe it's not as bad as the paper said." Josh shrugged, sipping his coffee.

"Oh, I think they accurately reported what happened."

"Well, he'll heal." Still no compassion.

"I certainly hope so."

"Now you don't have to see him." He had a satisfied grin on his lips before he sipped his coffee.

Angie sighed and sat back in her chair. "Was that the plan, Josh?"

"What plan?"

"You're plan. To take care of the situation." Her eyes were boring through him.

Josh's face froze.

"You did this, didn't you? You brutally beat a man old enough to be your father. Why would you do such a thing?" Maybe she had said too much. Somehow, she didn't care. It was how she felt. It was the truth.

"I'm telling you I didn't do it." Josh looked squarely into her eyes. He was a good liar.

"I don't believe you."

"What? Why would I beat up some old guy? I don't even know him." The sides of his face tightened significantly, and his brown eyes squinted in anger. He leaned toward her over the table. "I didn't do it." He banged the table with the flat of his hand for emphasis.

Angie felt nervous by his reaction. Clearly, he was angry with her, but that didn't change her feelings about the situation. In fact, it reinforced her belief that he was lying. She looked down into her lap, refraining from saying anything until he calmed down.

Josh leaned into the chairback and raised his arm to signal the server. The young man quickly came over. "Another shot of brandy."

"Yes, sir."

Angie remained silent, waiting to see what he did next.

When the server returned with the shot of brandy, Josh slung it down his throat, then looked across at Angie as he sipped his coffee. She felt like he was sending a message that she shouldn't mess with him.

"You want anything?" he finally asked.

"No."

Josh nodded satisfaction at her answer.

While he finished his coffee, Angie looked out at the restless sea. Lightning popped across the sky at a distance. The sea reminded her of their uneven relationship. If she could call this a relationship.

TWENTY

RACHEL AND JOE were having their morning coffee. It was Sunday, so they could be a bit more leisurely than on workdays. Joe had the paper spread around in front of him on the dining room table. Rufus walked over and placed his head on Joe's knee.

"Good boy, Rufus," he said, patting the dog's head.

The door opened leading to the hallway where Angie's bedroom was located.

"Morning," she said as she entered, being careful to close the door.

"Hi, honey," Rachel said. "There's coffee if you want it."

"Okay." Angie poured herself a cup from the decanter on the center of the table, adding stevia, a dash of vanilla flavored creamer, and sat in a chair.

"How was the date?" Joe asked.

Angie hesitated. "Okay."

"Just okay?" Rachel asked.

"Maybe not even," Angie said, slurping.

Joe looked over at his daughter, a question in his eyes.

She wasn't sure she wanted to give details about their

date. It had not ended well. Josh had driven her home after he finished his spiked coffee. After a silent ride, he let her out of the car at the curb by the entrance to the elevators. While he was parking his car, she made her way to the fourth floor before he returned. She also was reluctant to reveal what she knew about Josh. And what she suspected. At least not at this time.

"I blamed Josh for your disappearance, actually confronted him," her mother said. "I don't trust him."

"What do you think, Daddy?"

"I don't know. Your mother's the one with the intuition," he said, folding the section of the newspaper he was reading in half.

"I don't trust him, either. He lies." Angie admitted, sitting back in the chair with a sigh.

"How so?" Joe asked.

"Let's just say he lacks scruples."

Rachel and Joe exchanged looks.

Changing the subject, Joe said, "Are you going to church with us?"

"Sure, I'd like that. It wouldn't hurt me a bit."

Both parents smiled. Then they heard what sounded like someone crowing outside their door.

"What's that?" Joe asked, rising.

"It's probably Gladys crowing," Rachel said, as if this were normal. "I guess she's taken a liking to our door now."

Angie looked at her mother with a confused expression. "You know about this crowing?"

"It's nothing. Go get ready for church," Rachel said. "I'll have a talk with Gladys."

When the drummer laid out a few fancy drum rolls, Angie perked up. She was clearly enjoying herself, Rachel observed.

She would love for her daughter to attend church frequently. This was a good start.

On the way home, Angie chattered about the service. She liked the sermon, and the music was awesome, using that particular word to describe her experience. Rachel felt like her daughter might be turning over a new leaf. Not only was she working and seeking a better job, but she also enjoyed church. What had happened between Josh and her, she didn't know. But she didn't have to. She was satisfied that they were moving away from each other. She couldn't quite state what her objection was to Josh; she just knew he was bad news for her daughter. Her intuition was pinging.

"Joe, why don't we take Angie to see the house?"

"Yeah, we can do that," he said, turning to cross the bridge instead of driving into the condo parking lot. "You'll have to use your imagination. I have the upstairs torn up."

Joe parked the car beside the house, and the ladies got out of the car. After he unlocked the door, he swung it open for them to enter.

"This is cute," Angie said. "I can definitely see it as a B and B."

She continued into the dining room and kitchen. "This dining room is large enough so you could accommodate up to eight people in here. That's two per bedroom."

"Come upstairs," Rachel said.

The three walked to the second floor. Angie poked her head into the bathroom, which was filled with a toolbox and tools. Some paneling was leaned against the wall, covering the window.

"I like the tub," she said. "Nice touch for an old house." The clawfoot tub was in prime condition and would be the focal point of the room.

"I'm adding a bathroom in this bedroom," Joe said, walking to the room at the end of the hall.

"This is a big room," Angie said as she approached the bedroom. "You can easily add a bathroom."

She peeked inside each room until she came to the one closest to what was to be the main bath. "Oh, my, what is that?" She saw the shelves with the dolls staring out at them.

"Those are old dolls," Rachel said calmly. "They came with the house."

"Creepy," Angie said.

"See, Joe? Angie thinks they're creepy, too." Rachel felt vindicated.

"They're not creepy. They have character."

Rachel looked at her husband. "Joe, those are creepy dolls. Admit it."

"Not admitting anything."

Rachel rolled her eyes, as did Angie.

"I saw you two, the eye rolling stuff," he said, pointing at them.

"You're not planning to keep them, are you?" Angie asked.

"Why would I get rid of them?" Joe asked.

"I don't know, Daddy, because they might scare the customers?" She gave him one of those looks that said, this is so obvious, what are you thinking?

Joe shook his head. "Let's get out of here before the dolls get us." He smirked as he left the room.

"So, where'd you say you're going in our new car?" Rachel asked.

Angie grinned. "The hospital. I'm going to visit James."

"And you think that's a good thing to do?"

"Yes, I do. He was my customer; he got injured at my place of business. I think I owe him a visit." Angie slid her purse onto her arm.

Rachel had real concerns about this visit her daughter

thought was important. "What if he takes your visit the wrong way?"

"He won't. I'll explain."

"Are you feeling guilty?"

"No, responsible."

Rachel looked up at her daughter from the dining room table where she had resumed reading the Sunday paper. "Responsible?"

"I think Josh beat him up to send a message to keep away from me." Finally, the truth was out.

Rachel put the paper on the table. "That doesn't make you responsible if that's what happened. Why do you think Josh beat him up?"

"Because of certain things he said when we've been out. Like, 'I can talk to him, pay him a visit.' He seemed angry when I mentioned James' attention to me."

"You really think he's that kind of person?"

"Yes, I do." It appeared there was no doubt in her mind that Josh was a bad operator.

"I don't think you should see him again." She didn't want to be demanding, but this guy was bad news, in her opinion.

"I don't either. I've already decided I'm not going out with him again."

Rachel nodded her head. "Good."

TWENTY-ONE

ANGIE SAW the room number the nurse had given her posted on the door as she tried to ignore the antiseptic smell of the environment. She hesitated a moment, then walked into the hospital room. James was lying in bed, a cast on his arm and a bandage wrapped around his head. His eyes were closed as he rested. She noticed considerable swelling and bruising around his eyes, along with lacerations on the rest of his face. All sorts of tubes were attached to him, streaming from several clear bags elevated on a metal apparatus.

She stepped beside his bed, contemplating whether to sit in the chair or not. One of his eyes popped open.

"Angie," James said in a croaky voice without moving his lips. She sat in the chair.

"James, maybe you shouldn't talk." The man sounded as awful as he looked.

"I can talk. I sound funny, but I can still talk." Obviously, he was determined to have a conversation.

Angie noticed his lips still weren't moving when he spoke. Neither was the rest of his face.

"Is your jaw broken, James?"

"Yes."

"Oh, my. And your arm, I see."

"Yes. I have a concussion and brain damage." He spoke slowly, managing to get his words out despite his wired jaw.

"I am so sorry this happened to you." She meant every word in that sentence.

"So am I."

Angie took a deep breath before she began. "James, I feel like this is my fault. This shouldn't have happened to you."

"Not your fault. You didn't beat me up."

"That's true. But I think I know why this happened to you." The man had a right to know the identity of his attacker.

James' one eye blinked a few times before he focused on her. The other eye remained swollen shut.

"As I am sure you will remember, you were paying way too much attention to me at work," she said, looking at the man kindly. "It was inappropriate, and I didn't think I had done anything to encourage your persistence, gift, or large tips. So, at some point I mentioned you bothering me to my boyfriend." Angie sighed and shook her head. "I think he beat you up to send a message."

"I didn't know you had a boyfriend." His eye blinked rapidly as he stared at her.

"Maybe if I had told you, this wouldn't have happened," she said, looking sadly at him. "But it wasn't your business if I had a boyfriend."

James grunted his agreement. "But none of this is your fault. You are not to blame."

"I'm still sorry this happened to you."

"It's not your fault. The blame lays at the feet of the one who did this to me." His body did an involuntary shiver, then his head twitched to one side and back again.

"True."

"Who is my attacker?" James asked. "All I saw was a man dressed in black, and muscular. I didn't see his face clearly."

"That is definitely Josh. He always wears black. His name is Josh Brigham. He lives at the Breezeway Condominium. Unit 810."

"Would you write that down?"

"Sure." Angie reached for a notepad placed on the wheeled tray where his water container was located. She wrote the information on the pad with a pen from her purse. "I'll leave this attached to the pad, so it doesn't get lost."

"Thank you."

"Is there anything I can do? Is there something I can bring you?" Anything he wanted she would provide.

"Nothing," he said. "Well, maybe my phone."

"Of course." Angie retrieved the man's phone from the side table and placed it on the bed beside James.

"Thank you."

"You're welcome, James. It's the least I can do."

"Goodbye, sweet girl." With effort, James lifted one hand.

"Goodbye, James."

Angie left the hospital room and James fumbled with his phone, placing it on his chest. He was not going to let this young man get away with attacking him, leaving him for dead. He was a thug and deserved to be put behind bars before he killed someone. James extended his arm toward the notepad with the name of his attacker written on it. As his fingertips barely touched the pad, his arm fell back onto the bed. He tried again, raising his head slightly, but the effort was too great. His head fell back to the pillow. Suddenly, he felt a sharp pain zip into his temple. It was excruciating, causing him to breathe heavily. His hand blindly felt around for the call button as he lay with his eyes squeezed shut in pain. He needed help.

. . .

While Angie was loading the dishwasher, her eyes caught sight of Brian. He was scraping the griddle free from burnt on food with a spatula. She noticed he was not as heavy as he had been. While he would always be a large man, that was just the way he was built, he was thinner than when she had first come to work for him.

"Hey, Brian," she called out. "You losing weight or something?"

The man looked over her way and then turned back to his task. "Yeah, some."

"Good for you."

"Thanks. It crept up on me, the weight I mean. Too many fries," he said, dislocating a large spot of burnt food with the spatula. "Even started working out at the gym."

"Wow, Brian, I'm impressed."

The man smiled as he scraped. "Haven't seen James in lately. Wonder if he's out of the hospital?"

"I don't know." James was supposed to report her suspicions to the police. She had given him Josh's name and address. But she was not aware of any police coming around the condo to speak with Josh. She would know because her mother would definitely mention such a thing to her. They should have brought him in for questioning by now. She wondered why that hadn't happened?

"I'm taking my break and calling the hospital, Brian."

"Okay."

Angie slipped into the break room, pulling her phone from her pocket. When the operator answered her call, she asked about what room James was in. He had been in progressive care when she visited. By now, if he was still in the hospital, he should have been in a regular room.

"No, miss, I don't have a record of him being here currently," the woman said.

"Can you tell me if he's been released or is in rehab?"

"I'm afraid I can't give you that information. I'm sorry."

"Okay, well, thank you."

Angie walked back into the kitchen, standing near Brian. "He isn't there and they won't give me any details."

"He could be in rehab."

"They wouldn't tell me."

"He could be dead."

His words jolted her. "Dead? I hadn't thought of that."

"Check online. County death records."

"I will when I get home." Dead? Was it possible James had died?

Angie walked through the front door, calling out to her mother. "Hey, Mom, where are you?"

"In the bedroom."

Angie walked into the room where Rachel was making the bed. She looked at her mother with questions in her eyes.

"What's up?"

"Want to help me investigate something?"

"Sure. Like what?"

"James. To see if he's alive."

Rachel's face changed expression. "I see. Give me five and I'll meet you in your room."

Angie walked into the hallway, carefully keeping Precious from escaping to freedom. Once inside her bedroom, she opened her laptop and fired it up. Rachel entered shortly thereafter, carrying Precious in her arms, and nuzzling her face.

"I told you she's sweet," Angie said, tapping the keyboard with her fingertips.

"When she wants to be," Rachel said. "I think we need to let her roam more so she can get used to the dog and Benny. And they to her."

"I agree. Let's start today."

"Okay, after we get done here." Rachel sat on the edge of the bed. "Where do we begin?"

"I shared my suspicions about Josh with James, even gave him his name and address."

"Okay."

"That was a few days ago. I thought the police should have paid Josh a visit by now, don't you think? So, I called the hospital to find out if he was still there," Angie said, flicking her ponytail over her shoulder. "He wasn't there, and they wouldn't give me any information. So, I need to find out if he's alive."

"That shouldn't be hard," Rachel said. "Google his name. The county website or the newspapers should have obituaries posted."

Angie did exactly that, typing in James' full name. Being it was a common name, several James Marshalls popped up on the screen. Narrowing down the selection to deaths and then approximate age and a limited date range of death probability, she found a potential person.

"Here is the closest possibility if it's him. This is a news article." Angie said, clicking on the selection and reading aloud. "'A man named James C. Marshall, fifty-two, died in the hospital, as a result of brain damage.' Mom, that date is when I saw him at the hospital." The seriousness of the situation was written all over her face.

Her mother's eyes reflected her concern. "What you're saying is, he died after you talked to him."

"Yes. After I told him Josh beat him up. Actually, Josh murdered James now that this has happened."

"Maybe he had a reaction to that news, causing him to die." Rachel blinked a couple times at her daughter.

"Great. Now I am not only responsible for him getting

beat up, but for causing his death." Angie threw her one hand into the air. "He probably had a stroke or something."

"Don't blame yourself. You had to tell him."

"That's what I thought, but I didn't mean to kill him." Angie's eyes were round with worry.

"You didn't kill him, Angie. That was simply his bodily response after receiving a severe beating. You aren't to blame," Rachel said.

"Really?" Angie looked at her mother through hurting eyes. "I could have kept my suspicions to myself. I didn't have to tell him about Josh."

"Maybe not. But if Josh beat him up, the police need to know."

"But do they know? I keep expecting them to show up to arrest Josh, or at least haul him in for questioning," Angie said. "I don't think James told them."

"Then you have to."

"Me? Oh, no, I'm not doing that. Uh huh." Angie threw her hands into the air.

"They need to know. Josh needs to pay for this," Rachel insisted.

"What if it isn't Josh?"

A brief silence came between them. "What if it is?" Rachel said.

Angie looked helplessly at her mother.

"Pray about it, Angie."

"I will." Prayer was definitely on her agenda this evening.

TWENTY-TWO

"OKAY, you little devil, get out here and mingle," Rachel said, standing beside the open door to the hallway. "This is your big chance, so don't blow it."

The white fluffball waltzed into the dining room, flinging her tail about as she met the challenge. With her nose in the air to smell the surroundings, she meekly pranced forward between the observers.

"Good girl," Angie said.

"Yeah, stay good," Rachel said.

"Don't mess with Benny," Joe said.

They heard Benny spit after the mention of his name and saw him dive under the bed to hide. Rufus cautiously came near the prissy cat, walking ever so slowly with his head down. The two touched noses, each backing away afterwards. Precious continued to investigate her surroundings, eventually sitting on the arm of the couch so she could look outside at the balcony.

"Hmm, not too bad; so far so good," Rachel said.

"Why don't we let her stay out until something happens?"

Angie asked. "They will never adjust if she's hidden in the bedroom."

"Probably true," Joe said.

"It's okay with me. She has to adjust and so do the other two," Rachel said.

Precious looked over at the family as if she knew they were talking about her. She made a little purp noise suggesting she was in agreement.

The rest of the evening went well. Rufus seemed to be all right with the cat. He occasionally walked over to smell her. That was fine with Precious, unless he drooled on her, then she took exception, hissing at the big dog. Everything was going along just fine, until Benny decided to come out from under the bed. He boldly walked over to Precious and growled his disapproval. Precious responded with her own low rumble.

"Knock it off!" Angie said. "Behave, both of you."

The two cats stopped their utterings and looked up at Angie. She pointed her finger at the cats. The pointed finger trick worked very well with Rufus but did not have quite the same response from the cats. They slinked away from each other after a few moments, reclining on opposite sides of the room where they could watch each other.

"They'll be fine." Rachel had been observing the exchange. "Let them work it out."

"Okay." Angie's phone rang, so she looked to see who the caller was. Seeing it was Josh calling, she did not answer. Maybe he finally took the hint. After all, this was his third call to her that she had not answered. "Give it up, dude."

That night Angie went down on her knees in prayer. She hadn't been on her knees in a long time, unless while practicing yoga. She hadn't forgotten about God. She had just wandered into Eastern philosophy and beliefs. Was that so bad? Hmm, according to her early teachings, yes, it was. But here she was now, asking for help. From God. What was she to do? The police needed to know who attacked James. That was only right. If James hadn't passed on her suspicions to the police, she had to. It was the moral thing to do. But thoughts of Josh's angry reactions flashed in her thoughts. Did she have the courage to inform the police, knowing he had a temper, knowing he would react negatively? Maybe even violently.

Angie finished asking for help from God, then rose and climbed into bed. Precious immediately snuggled beside her. "Precious puddin', what is mommy to do?" She turned to her side and Precious molded herself next to her. As she drifted off to sleep, Angie felt she had the answer.

Rachel knocked on Loretta's door the following morning. After a moment, the door opened. She looked better than the last time Rachel had seen her in the hospital. Today she wore a housedress in a lovely shade of rose. Her hair, while not fixed in her usual poufy updo, was at least neatly drawn back into a low chignon.

"Rachel, come in," she said, stepping back from the door. "Come sit in the living room."

"You look so much better," Rachel said with a big smile.

"Well, when one spends time in the hospital, they're guaranteed to get a rest – if they can sleep through the racket in the halls."

Rachel sat on the white silk couch, scooting back so she was comfortable. "How long have you been home?"

"About ten days. Didn't Ruby tell you?" Loretta sat next to Rachel.

"No. She must have wanted you all to herself."

Loretta laughed, her beautiful blue eyes crinkling at the edges. "She has been here every day since my return. I don't know what I would do without my Ruby."

"I am so happy you two made up and are friends now."

"Sisters. More like sisters," she said. "We're too old to have issues. Time is short. We can't waste time."

"No, I guess not."

"While I was in rehab, Ruby came to see me almost every day," she said, brushing a stray hair out of her face. "That's saying something since her ex-husband has come back into her life."

"That's wonderful. How is their relationship going? Ruby hasn't paid me a visit in the office to chat as of late."

"Oh, I've never known her to be so happy. She is just beaming every time I see her. Bob is having quite an impact on her life," Loretta said, smiling sweetly. "But tell me, how is your life running?"

"Not bad at all."

"Are you still going to church?"

"Oh, I wouldn't miss it. I also attend Bible study," Rachel said. "Angie has been going to church with us, which pleases us so much."

"That's wonderful, Rachel." Loretta fussed with the sleeve on her housedress. "I once told you that you needed to go to church. Remember? You looked at me like I'd lost my marbles."

"Yes, I guess I did. But I didn't see the need back then. Now I understand."

"You're God's daughter; His precious child."

Rachel smiled at the old woman. "Now I know."

The family sat down for dinner, Joe said grace, and everyone dove into their meal. Joe recognized the worry on his daughter's face. "What's wrong?"

Angie looked at her father for advice. "Josh. And James. James died as a result of his beating from Josh. I think I have to tell the police I suspect Josh for having beat him up."

Joe looked sympathetically at her, placing his fork back on his plate. "Tell the police, Angie. Let them determine if he did it or not. If he's innocent, that's good; if not, then he will be arrested."

"Daddy, he is an angry man." Angie stopped eating her dinner, pushing her plate away. "He could come after me next. I don't want to get beat up, or worse."

Joe carefully evaluated the situation, looking at his plate for a few seconds before he spoke. "You have to tell the police. But also mention your fears of his reaction."

"Of course."

"They might offer protection."

"Maybe."

"But you have to tell them."

"Okay, Daddy." When her father said this, she felt it was confirmation of what God wanted her to do.

TWENTY-THREE

BRIAN BROUGHT two cups of coffee to the booth where Angie sat. He positioned himself across from her, looking at her concerned face. "You wanted to tell me something?"

"Yes. I went to visit James in the hospital."

"Yeah, so you said."

"I did it because I felt responsible." She took a sip of coffee. "I don't know if I told you that or not."

He gave her a curious expression. "How in the world are you responsible?"

"He got beat up because of me. Josh was jealous, or over-protective, I'm not sure which. Maybe just nasty," she said, bringing the cup to her lips again. "If I hadn't mentioned the attention James was giving me, Josh wouldn't have known anything. So, I'm responsible."

Brian shook his head. "I don't agree. Josh is responsible if he's the one who did it. He chose to react with violence. He's responsible, not you."

"Oh, he did it, all right. No one else would have responded like that. And not many people knew about

James." She placed the cup on the table. "I went to the police today."

"Really? Why?"

"I suspect James wasn't able to tell the police what I told him about Josh." She paused a second and resumed. "So, I felt I had to inform them."

Brian looked at her with respect. "Wow, that was brave."

"You think? I'm not so sure. It might have been a stupid move." Angie coiled a lock of her ponytail around her finger. "What if Josh comes after me?"

Brian looked at her carefully. "That's a thought. But you live in a secure building, and when you come here, you have me."

Angie smiled at her employer. "Oh, that's sweet. I appreciate that very much. But he does live in the same building as me. I am accessible."

"And then there's that. What did the police say?"

"They said they would investigate my suspicions, no problem there," she said. "No one else has popped up on their radar as suspects."

"What about protecting you?"

"Well, he'd have to do something for them to assign a person to protect me. He is innocent until proven guilty, and it may not be him, they said." She shrugged her shoulders and took another sip of coffee.

"If they arrest him, he'll bond out, more than likely, and then he's free to attack you," Brian said.

"Yes, true. Maybe he's that bold. I don't know. Obviously, I don't have all the answers, Brian. I didn't know what to do." She turned the cup around between her hands in nervous frustration before she took some sips. "We'll just have to see how it works out."

Brian stood, looking down at Angie. "I don't like it. You could be in danger."

"Yes, I know, but I felt I had to tell the police about Josh. I thought about it a lot and finally I felt God wanted me to do this." Her blue eyes looked up at her boss. "By the way, you've lost more weight, haven't you?"

"You're changing the subject," he said. "But, yes, I have lost more weight. I'm not eating fries and I only eat half the bun."

"That's terrific, Brian." She really did admire the man. He was a wonderful boss. And he was becoming a friend.

"Thanks. No girl's going to be interested in me if I'm fat," he said, patting his flattened stomach.

"You weren't that fat. You're a big guy, that's all, and you have a kind heart." She smiled at the man. "I'm sure a girl will see how nice you are soon."

"Thanks. I have my eye on someone." Brian shrugged. "So, maybe…"

"That's great. I'm happy for you."

"Thanks."

Penelope took Alfred's hand and dragged him through Rachel's office door.

"Hi, guys. How are you?" Rachel put down her pen and gave the couple her full attention.

"Fine," Penelope said. Alfred grunted his agreement. "Alfred here needs you to notarize something."

"Certainly, I'd be happy to." Rachel opened a drawer to locate her stamp and register. "What am I signing?"

Alfred finally got his nerve up and spoke. "I'm giving my car to my son. His went kerflooey."

"That's nice of you, Alfred."

"I don't drive much. I don't need a car now with Penelope driving me around." Alfred looked over at the old woman and nodded.

"He shouldn't be driving anyway," Penelope said, pulling

the arms of her sweater closer to her hands. "His skills aren't what they used to be. Always slamming on his brakes at the last minute. Scares me to death."

"I see," Rachel said, looking at the registration form Alfred handed her. "Okay, Alfred, sign here and write a date. Fill in your son's name here." She pointed to the areas she spoke of with the end of the pen.

Alfred wrote in the proper locations. "Penelope, you need to sign here as a witness." Rachel again pointed to indicate where. She then signed and stamped everything, recording the transaction in her register. "Penelope, please sign my register as the witness."

"Yes, dear. Thank you, Rachel," Penelope said, signing her name. "You must have spoken with Ethel."

"Why do you say that?"

"Because she's wearing a coverup when she walks around the building."

"Oh. I'm glad she's doing that." Rachel had not spoken to her about covering her pudgy body when in a two piece. "I think she did that on her own because I haven't said anything to her."

"Well, anyway, she's covering herself now," Penelope said with an approving nod.

"Why don't you make friends with her? She needs companionship now that she's a widow."

"Me?"

"Why not you?"

"I, I don't know. I guess I could." Penelope looked at her as if the thought had never entered her mind.

"You could benefit from having a friend, don't you think?" Rachel had never seen the old lady associating with anyone in the building, except Alfred, but that was recent.

"Okay, Rachel. I'll do it. And thank you."

Alfred added his appreciation as well, and the couple left the office.

Later, when Rachel entered the empty apartment, Precious was having a happy time sharpening her claws on the corner of the sofa. Squatted in front, she flashed her impressive tail in the air as she continued to impart damage to the fabric.

"Precious! Bad girl!" Rachel ran toward the cat, waving her arms. "Get away from my couch, you hussy!"

Precious wandered off, still flashing her tail around, giving Rachel a sour look over her shoulder.

"Brat."

Rachel sat at the table while she went through the mail. Mostly garbage for the trash collectors. Why did every business feel the need to send out an endless supply of advertisements? Then she heard a crash. Looking behind her, she saw dear Precious coyly sitting on the arm of the couch. Below her was a crystal vase that had been sitting on the table beside the couch, now broken to smithereens. The cat looked around like she had no clue what had happened.

"Precious! You brat! What next?" she said, rising from the chair. "Get out of here. Go to your room."

Precious made a beeline into the hallway leading toward the bedroom. Rachel looked after her. "How can one cat be so destructive?" This wasn't the first time she had taken a fancy to knocking something from its place. There had been other incidents before this one, like her perfume atomizer being pawed off the bureau. That had been a smelly mess. The scent of Chanel No.5 had permeated the entire unit for a week. All of the shenanigans had occurred after they had decided to allow Precious free reign in their home. Rachel was regretting that decision.

Angie walked into the home, looking at her mother standing in the middle.

"What's up?"

"Your cat just pushed over my crystal vase. Look." Rachel pointed at the crystal fragments on the floor.

"I'm sorry, Mom." Angie walked over to look at the damage. "Gee, I really am sorry. I'll clean it up." Angie walked toward the storage closet to get a dustpan and broom.

"This isn't the first time. Remember the matching vase? And the atomizer?" Rachel asked. "Does this cat hate me?"

"I don't think it's a matter of hate or like. She just enjoys knocking things off tables." Angie bent to the floor to gather the broken pieces.

"She needs to behave better."

"She's a cat, Mom. This is what cats do."

"Not all cats. Benny has never purposely knocked over something. Never."

"That you know of."

Rachel shot her daughter a look that said she expected agreement. Then the buzzer rang. She walked over to the phone and pushed the intercom button. "Yes?" The public infrequently buzzed her for entry. Sometimes she allowed it, other times, no.

"It's the Daytona Police. We need entry to speak with one of your tenants," the masculine voice said.

"Which tenant?"

"A Josh Brigham, unit 810."

"Oh, yes. I'll buzz you in." Rachel pushed the button again to allow entry.

When she turned around, Rachel saw the look on her daughter's face. It was clearly one of fear. "It's okay. At least we got a warning. We know he will be asked questions and can have our guard up."

"I'll have to be extra careful every time I step outside the door." Angie gave a heavy sigh.

"Your father can take you to work and bring you home."

"That might be a good idea," she said, standing with the dustpan in hand.

"Yes, it is." Her Mama Hen instincts kicked in. She didn't want to ever repeat the recent calamity she and Joe experienced when their daughter went missing.

TWENTY-FOUR

THE NEXT MORNING Rachel and Angie sat side by side at the dining room table. The laptop was placed there, and Angie was ready for business.

"Bring up Google," Rachel said.

"Got it." Angie looked to her mother for more direction.

"Type in the dad's name. John Brigham."

"Done. Lots of them. How do we know which to pick?" Again, she looked to her mother.

"Click that one, the name associated with Nevada. See what happens."

"Still quite a few."

"Pick one at random and let's see." One of them had to be their John Brigham.

After going through six John Brighams in Nevada, they found one with a criminal record. Almost. This particular man had several run ins with the law, but never was convicted of anything.

"What were some of the charges?" Rachel asked, leaning against the back of the chair.

"One is illegal gambling. Illegal? In Nevada? I thought everybody gambled in Nevada." Angie continued scrolling.

"I'm sure there are laws governing the gambling. Maybe he broke one," Rachel said.

Angie dove deeper into the files. "Look at this one. He beat the charge. Oddly, for a botched arrest. How convenient. Like father, like son." She gave her mother a knowing look. "Is it possible to arrange a botched arrest?"

"Maybe if you know people in the police department," her mother said.

"Huh. Interesting." Angie kept digging for several minutes while Rachel looked on at the screen.

"I'm seeing a lot of gambling charges. Operating an illegal poker game behind a normal business. Orchestrating gambling parties in hotel rooms. Threatening a dealer. Except, look at this, it wasn't John doing the threatening. It says, 'His associate threatened,' etc. Holy Moley. Maybe that was Josh?" Angie looked at her mother with big eyes. "I wonder about the other states where Mr. Brigham has 'business?'"

"Keep looking. It's getting interesting."

"So, what have you ladies been doing today?" Joe asked as he reached for the salad dressing.

Mother and daughter exchanged looks. Rachel spoke first. "We've been researching John Brigham. Turns out he has a long history of arrests and one prison sentence for gambling charges."

"In several states. But he manages to get off most times due to botched arrests. Like Josh did," Angie said in between munching her salad. "We suspect that Josh is his 'enforcer,' as in, he roughs up people who owe his dad money."

Joe looked surprised. "Gambling? It's legal in some states, such as Florida."

"This is gambling in hotel rooms, private homes, and so forth, where there isn't a license purchased or a legally run operation with permits," Rachel said. "All under the table."

"And Josh is an enforcer? You suspect," Joe said, mixing his salad with his fork.

"Stretching the imagination to fill in the blanks, we are guessing when a contact sets up gambling for Mr. Brigham, they owe him money. If they don't pay, well, use your imagination," Angie said.

Joe looked over at his wife. "Really? And they live in our condo?"

"Unfortunately." Rachel shrugged her shoulders. "They could be holding games in their unit for all I know."

"I haven't noticed any unusual number of people entering the building," Joe said.

"Maybe they keep gambling away from their home," Angie said, reaching for a chicken breast. "And I hope they do. We don't need that here."

"No, we don't," Joe said, sliding a piece of chicken into his mouth. "So, this means you were seeing an enforcer, Angie. That's one for the record."

"I didn't know he was an enforcer, Dad," Angie said, shaking her head. "And I'm not seeing him now. Besides, the police are interested in him."

"He's dangerous," Rachel said. "You need to take her to work tomorrow, Joe."

"No problem," Joe said.

Brian was flipping burgers on the grill when Angie walked into the kitchen after Joe dropped her off. Bonnie was loading the dishwasher.

"Hey, guys," Angie said.

"Hey," Bonnie said, with a quick smile.

"You are the most punctual employee I have," Brian said. "You're never late, usually early."

"Isn't that the way an employee should be?" Angie said, taking an apron off the hook.

Bonnie walked away. She was rarely on time.

Brian grinned. "Yes, that's the preferable behavior. Thanks for being a good employee."

"Of course. Thanks for being a good boss."

Bonnie returned with bags of buns in her arms. "Hey, Brian, you've lost more weight."

Angie looked over at her boss. His chest was definitely larger than his waist and his arms had noticeably grown in size. His paunch was a thing of the past.

"Yeah, Brian, you have lost a lot. Good for you," Angie said.

"I've been working out," Brian said.

"It shows," Bonnie said.

"It sure does." Angie smiled with appreciation at her boss. He had turned into a hunk.

"Okay, enough, you're embarrassing me," Brian said, sliding the spatula into a hole beside the griddle. "Get to work."

Brian was a modest man, and a little on the quiet side. At least he appeared that way to Angie. She didn't know much about him, only that he was single and had grown up in Daytona Beach. After all these months, she wasn't even sure where he lived.

Later that night, when they were cleaning up the kitchen after closing, Angie took the opportunity to ask Brian some questions.

"Brian, where are you from?" Angie asked as she finished distributing clean utensils into their proper containers.

"Miami. My parents moved here when I was three." He was doing the final cleanup on the grill.

"You've been here a long time. Where do you live?" She moved over to a counter with a rag.

"Why? You planning to visit me?" he asked with a grin.

"No, just curious." She stopped cleaning the counter and stared at him, rag in hand.

"I have a little house on the beach in South Daytona. Nothing to brag about, but it's mine and paid for." He untied his apron and flung it into the laundry bag near the dishwasher.

"Must be nice living on the beach."

"Yeah, I like it. Very quiet at night."

"I live on the beach, too, but four floors up. Not quite the same," she said, untying her apron after she tossed a well-used rag into the trash.

"You want to come over and see my place sometime?" His handsome face had hope written all over it.

"Sure, that would be nice," she said, tossing her apron into the laundry bag.

"Saturday? I could throw a steak on the grill after we get off here," he said, looking at her a bit sheepishly. The question in his blue eyes gave his face a little boy appearance that she found appealing.

"Okay, that would be nice."

"All right, then," he said, shoving his hands into his pockets to get his keys. "Saturday."

TWENTY-FIVE

JOHN BRIGHAM WALKED into Rachel's office. His energy filled the room, making Rachel uncomfortable.

"Mrs. Barnes, I need a word with you."

"You can call me Rachel," she said, trying to appear calm.

"Whatever. What is this outlandish charge your daughter has levied against my son?" The man's face was dark as he hovered over her desk. "I won't stand for false accusations from a silly girl."

"My daughter is not silly. And she's a woman, not a girl." *And here we go.*

"Semantics," he said, interrupting. "She is stirring up trouble and I won't tolerate it. I demand you have her withdraw her accusation."

Rachel's eyebrows rose, along with her temper. "Demand? Who are you to make demands on my family?"

"I could be your worst enemy," he said, leaning downward with his hands resting on the desk, closer to where she sat in her chair. "Don't make me do something both of us will regret."

"You have said enough. It's time for you to leave my office," she said in a strong voice touched with anger. "I will not allow you to threaten me. Don't come back here again."

The man smirked at her. "Have a good day." John left the office, slamming the door.

Rachel was shaking. Never had she been threatened in such a manner. He had no right to treat her as he had, but his behavior did have the intended affect. She was scared.

When Joe walked into the office, he knew immediately something was wrong with his wife. The recent experience was written all over her face.

"What happened?"

"That awful man just threatened me." She clutched the armrests of the chair with both hands.

"What man?"

"John Brigham."

"What was he doing here?

"Telling me, no, *demanding* that I make Angie retract her accusation toward his son." Rachel sat before her husband, looking wide eyed and nervous.

"What did you do?"

"I told him to leave and not come back. He said he could be my worst enemy, Joe."

"I think we need to let the detective assigned to this case know what happened." Joe's expression and entire demeanor looked serious. "Now."

"Okay." She trusted Joe's decision.

After dialing the phone and her call being passed to several people, the detective assigned to the death case of James Marshall answered. Rachel explained what had just happened.

"Mrs. Barnes, I am making note of this. Please let me know should another incident occur." His voice sounded concerned while retaining a professional tone.

"I hope another incident doesn't occur," she said. "But what can I do to avoid it? I was threatened. I was hoping for protection."

"We will contact Mr. Brigham and advise him to cease all verbal threats to you. Once he knows the police are aware of his behavior, that will probably end the threats," he said. "I'm sorry you are in this situation. I suggest you avoid this man and his son as best you can."

"Well, of course. I'm not an idiot," she said. "Except, we all live in the same building. We do run into each other."

"I can only suggest avoiding them. I can't put a guard outside your door. Let me know should anything else occur."

"I will." *If I'm alive to do it.*

Rachel picked up her fan and vigorously waved it in the air to cool herself. Stress exacerbated her hot flashes. And she was stressed. Threats to herself and daughter had a tendency to lead to a stressful reaction. *Those Brighams!*

Rachel was so glad she lived on the fourth floor and not the eighth. It would be easier to avoid John and Josh when she had to leave her unit. She also could observe from her office who was near the elevator before she ventured out and got on. She didn't want to be killed in the elevator by one of her enemies. And then, at times the thought came to her that maybe she was being melodramatic. But she had received a threat. That was not the product of an overactive imagination. So, caution was the word for the day. Every day.

She glanced from side to side to make sure no one was standing nearby her unit as she exited the elevator. With key in hand, she quickly unlocked the door, entered, and locked the door behind her. Safe. She spied Precious sitting in the middle of the living room, looking innocent.

"What have you been up to? Break anything lately?"

The cat flicked its bushy tail, sauntering off in another direction.

Rachel made herself some tea and walked over to the balcony. She sat in one of the cushy chairs and contentedly sipped her drink. Peace at last. All of this stress was not good for her diabetes. She had been feeling faint at times, and she knew it was from stress. Her diet was very good since her diagnosis. She did not want to exacerbate her disease, so she was careful with what she ate. And her medication. She was a good patient.

Reaching for her Bible, Rachel thumbed over to the concordance. She looked up peace and found something in John 14:27. "Peace I leave with you; my peace I give you. I do not give to you as the world gives. Do not let your hearts be troubled and do not be afraid."

Do not be afraid.

No fear. Fear has no hold on me. Can't touch me. His arms surround me. I am safe.

Rachel placed the Bible on the side table, glancing out at the pool. First, she saw Ethel's curly blue hair bobbing as she walked toward a chaise lounge. The woman peeled off her white coverup before she sat her plump body down. Penelope came walking along, as she often did around the pool. From her vantage point, it appeared Penelope struck up a conversation with Ethel, and Ethel was receptive. *Wonderful*! The next thing she knew, Ethel stood and put on her coverup, then the two women started walking around the pool. Together. A friendship was born.

Ruby walked into Rachel's office, holding Loretta's hand.

"Ladies! I'm so glad to see the two of you out and about this morning," she said rising from her chair.

"We're just out for a stroll, maybe go to the grocery," Ruby said, looking at her friend with care beaming from her eyes.

"Yes, Ruby and I decided I needed to get out some,"

Loretta said, sitting in the only chair intended for visitors. She looked almost normal to Rachel. Today she was in one of her classic pantsuits, a yellow one, and her hair was pulled into a low chignon, not her usual updo. But she looked put together and dignified, not like a sick patient.

"I think she's able to go to the grocery," Ruby said, looking down at Loretta as she stood beside her. "She's out of most food and needs to put some weight on, don't you think?"

"Well," Rachel really didn't want to criticize the old lady after she'd been in such dire health. "She might need a couple pounds after her pneumonia bout. But she looks great to me."

"I feel so much better, Rachel. My strength is coming back and I'm starting to feel like I want to do things again."

"That's wonderful, Loretta." She liked hearing the positive attitude.

"Well, we just wanted to stop by on our way out," Ruby said. "We knew you'd want to know how our girl here is doing."

"Yes, of course, I do. And I can see you're doing great." Rachel walked over to open the door for the two friends. "I'm so glad you stopped by."

Loretta rose from her chair slowly, taking Ruby's hand for support as she walked to the door. "Bye, dear."

"Bye, ladies."

"See you," Ruby said as she led Loretta out the door.

"Ready to lock up," Brian called out to the staff. He had been hustling everyone more than usual in order to leave his place of business in a timely manner. It was obvious to Angie that he wanted to get on with the night ahead. The grilled steak at his place. Their first date, or so she gathered. What else could she call it?

Once outside in the parking lot, Brian motioned toward his car. "That's mine." Angie looked over to see a souped-up classic Camaro. Bright metallic green. It was fine in appearance.

Angie was impressed. "Wow, that's some car."

"My pride and joy. I've worked on this baby for years," he said, opening the door for her. "She's hand-polished. And has leather seats, too."

That wasn't all. The interior was fitted with a leather steering wheel, custom stereo, and speakers, not to mention the plush carpeting. And a gold tone cross hung from the rearview mirror. Obviously, he loved his car.

"Very nice, Brian," she said as he opened his door.

"Thanks."

They drove down A1A for a few miles before they entered South Daytona. It wasn't long from there that he pulled into a driveway that was hardly visible from the road. Large seagrass sprouted on both sides as they drove down to the garage. It was separate from the cottage-style house, sitting to the right side of it. Brian tapped the opener to a secure place to keep a classic vehicle from the salt air.

They walked to the front door of the house as Brian clicked his key ring to close the garage doors. The cottage was painted a soft aqua and had white hurricane shutters and an aluminum roof. Angie thought it was cute. When they walked inside, Angie was surprised to see how modern it was. The entire living area was wide open. Talk about open concept! Although it was a small house, the openness gave it a much larger feel. She could see the kitchen from the front door, and it was all white. A small wooden table with four chairs stood to the left of the kitchen. To the right of the front door, a leather loveseat and matching sofa were positioned to form a corner, with a large rough wooden table being used as a coffee table in front. Of course, a huge wide screen TV was attached to the wall.

"Down here's the bedroom." Brian led the way down a short hallway off the living room to the bedroom, with Angie following. It was painted a similar color to the exterior and had an attached bathroom. An en suite, no less. A glass enclosed shower glistened at her. It had what appeared to be rock tiling and a fancy waterfall showerhead. The counter had two sinks and great lighting to apply makeup. Except, there wasn't a woman living here. Just Brian.

When she reentered the bedroom, Angie noticed the long sliding closet doors. "Wow, lots of closet space."

"Yeah, look," Brian said as he slid half the doors open. What was revealed was a grouping of wooden shelves and drawers. "And over here," he said, sliding open the other half, "is the walk-in area."

"This is amazing," Angie said. Each side was lined in wood with a long area for hanging clothes, with shelves above. "It's so custom."

"I designed it myself and built most of it." It was obvious he was proud of his work.

"Really?"

"Yeah, and I did most of the work in the rest of the house, too."

"Who knew I had such a talented boss?" she said with a smile.

"Okay, let's get out of here or we won't be eating any steak," he said with a satisfied grin.

"Oh, yes, and now onto Chef Brian demonstrating another of his many talents, the art of steak grilling," she said playfully as they walked down the hall to the kitchen. "I didn't eat anything in preparation for this wonderful meal you're going to prepare. It had better be good!"

Brian laughed. "Okay, prepare to be amazed. This is my best talent, my expertise." On this matter, Brian was obviously not shy about boasting.

"I can hardly wait." Angie sat down on a bar stool near the counter, anxious to eat his magnificent steak.

TWENTY-SIX

SOMEONE RANG the doorbell to Rachel's unit. It took some time for her to reach the door. She had been taking a shower and had to grab her bathrobe to be presentable.

"LuAnn! Come in." She stepped back from the door to allow her to enter.

"I didn't want to bother you, but I didn't want to wait till the morning, either," LuAnn said, pulling at her sideways ponytail lying over her shoulder.

"It's okay. Come sit in the living room."

They walked over to the couch and sat beside each other. LuAnn looked at her with a peculiar expression. "What's up?" Rachel asked.

"The band wants to go on the road."

"That's a bad thing?"

"Well, we'd make more money. That part isn't bad."

"So, where's the problem?"

"We have to travel. A lot. Too much." LuAnn shot her a pouty expression.

"Oh, I see. You don't want to?"

"I did the road thing years ago. It was fun when I was in

my twenties or even in my thirties, to some extent. But I have a home now. I have friends. You guys are my family. I don't want to go on the road." LuAnn looked at her like she expected an answer to her dilemma to be forthcoming.

"Gee, girl, I don't know what to say. I see your point. Can't say I blame you." Rachel looked at her friend closely. There was more to this predicament. "If you don't go, what happens to your relationship with Derks?"

"We won't see each other, obviously, for who knows how long. That's not a good thing for a relationship."

Rachel remembered LuAnn's sad love stories of cheating spouses when she was on the road before. "And what will you do for income if your band is traveling?" Rachel tucked her feet under the robe.

"That's another problem. I'd have to find a gig. I can do that, but it's not what I want. Not at all," she said, her drawl becoming heavier from anxiety. "I like our setup now. The band, me and Derks, all together."

"Honey, I don't have an answer for you. There is no simple answer. Have you talked to Derks about this?" He was the one she needed to talk to about this situation, not her.

"Yes. He's all fired up to go," she said, with obvious sadness in her voice. "He hasn't been on the road as extensively as me. He thinks it sounds exciting. You know he's a little younger than me?"

That was news to Rachel. LuAnn looked younger than her years, so it was not a surprise she was seeing a younger man. It seemed the thing women did lately. "No, I didn't."

"Yes, about ten years," she said, tossing her hands into the air. "What can I say? I'm attracted to a younger guy. Lots of women my age are nowadays."

"It seems so. Is he certain to go with the band? Even if you don't?"

"I think so. He doesn't know the problems, so it all sounds

good to him." She puckered her lips downward, giving herself a strange expression.

"When I have problems with no answers, I always pray for an answer. It works for me," Rachel said, patting the hand LuAnn had resting on her knee, all sparkly with glitter on her long nails. "Try that and see what happens."

LuAnn squeezed the hand sitting on hers. "I'll give it a shot, sweetie. Okay, I'll leave you now to finish what you started," she said, standing. "You can't cook dinner dressed like that."

"Oh, no?" That was exactly her plan.

While the steaks sizzled on the outdoor grill, Brian set the picnic table for their dinner. Nothing was fancy, like at the restaurant Josh had taken her to, everything was comfortable and homey. Sitting at a picnic table looking at the ocean close up, was paradise to Angie. She felt relaxed. And she didn't feel the need to impress Brian. He was already impressed. If she dripped grease on her top, he wouldn't care.

"Okay, I've got everything out here we need. Salad, dressing, iced tea, and no ketchup."

"Ketchup?" She didn't understand the reference.

"Some people put ketchup on steak. I don't allow it. Not when I'm cooking the steak."

"I understand. I never use anything but salt on my steak. And pepper when cooking."

"Good woman," he said in appreciation. "Sit down, the feast is about to begin."

Angie stepped between the bench and table as she sat facing the ocean. It was romantically illuminated by a full moon. There were two candles to assist with lighting the table. Brian joined her after he set the plate holding the smoking steak in front of her.

"Do you want to say grace or should I?" he asked.

"Oh, I think you should." Angie was impressed. None of her previous boyfriends ever said grace, especially Josh. Only her dad led grace at the table.

After Brian finished grace, he told Angie to help herself to salad. He sliced the steak while she drizzled dressing on her tossed salad. When he finished, she leaned back so he could place a chunk on her plate. It looked marvelous.

"Oh, Brian. Wow!" she said, her speech garbled by a mouth full of delectable meat. "This is fantastic."

"Thank you." He poured dressing on his salad and tossed it around with his fork. "It's an old family recipe."

"I didn't know there were family recipes for steak."

"There probably aren't. It's in the technique, and that's my secret."

"Oh, really? You have secrets?" she teased.

"Only this one." He chuckled as he looked to his side at her.

"That's okay. I don't have to know as long as you continue cooking steak for me," she said with a grin.

"Woman, that is not a problem." Brian smiled broadly.

"I cook, some. I'm not great or anything. Not as good at you, and I certainly can't begin to touch your talent in cooking steak." She sipped her iced tea in between talking.

"That's okay. I'm sure you have other talents," he said, popping a piece of steak into his mouth.

"Yeah? I don't know what they are. Still trying to figure that one out." Angie really didn't know where she was going with her life. She hadn't had much time to job search since working with Brian and didn't really know what she wanted to do. She had a bunch of degrees that didn't add up to much of a resume for a specific career. This was her first job, at a burger joint. And she was twenty-five. That wasn't saying much for herself.

"You said you lived in ashrams for a while. How'd that happen?" he asked, slicing off a bite of meat.

"I got interested in Eastern religions, meditation, and yoga. I was in Massachusetts at the time and had just finished up a degree at a college. From there I was able to move into an ashram. When the opportunity came along to go to India, I jumped at the chance. A foreign country? Study with a guru?" she said, putting her fork down to emphasize her words with both her hands moving in the air like birds. "I was hooked, so off I went with some people in the ashram. We were there about three months, traveling from one ashram to another."

"How did you afford that?"

"If you work in the ashrams, you can stay for free. I helped out some in the kitchen, mostly cleaning, and in the office." She picked up her knife to slice more steak.

Brian nodded his head as he chewed. "That's cool. But how did you afford 'stuff?' Toothpaste, lipstick, a ticket to India?"

Angie felt uncomfortable. She reached back for her ponytail and twirled it around one finger, then looked sheepishly at Brian. "Well, hmm, you won't think bad of me?"

"Of course not."

She released her ponytail and dropped her hands to her lap. "I was a muse."

"A what?"

"A muse. A source of artistic inspiration. It's when something about a person, usually a woman, inspires an artist's creativity. So, they paint that person. She's a muse. She gets painted." Angie rattled off the meaning of the word like it was a common vocation.

"Let me get this straight; you posed for an artist?" Brian

shot her a curious look. "Because you somehow inspired this artist person and he, I assume it was a he, painted you?"

"Yes. Exactly."

"And he paid you?"

"Yes. Quite well, actually."

Brian looked at her with growing curiosity. "I've never heard of such a thing, except maybe back in high school during art class. And I've never known a muse, either."

"Now you do," she said, spreading her hands in the air.

"Did you pose in the nude?"

"Never! It was always discrete. Mostly, I wore normal clothes. Sometimes I posed outside, sometimes in his studio. A couple times I wore a bathing suit when at the shore. Whatever the situation called for. And I didn't have a relationship with him, either. It wasn't like that. Just a business arrangement." She stopped talking and looked to see his reaction to what she had said.

Brian didn't speak quickly enough for Angie. She was worried he was upset about her previous form of income. "Brian, are you upset with me?"

"No, I'm just trying to take it all in." His slight smile made her relax a little. "So, tell me what happened after India."

"Eventually, we went to an ashram north of London and stayed there for a while. I adore London," she said, stuffing another bite of meat into her mouth, some of the juice shining on her lips. "But it's incredibly expensive to live there and buy things. So, we came back to Massachusetts for a while."

"And then you came here?"

"No, I went with another girl to California and stayed at an ashram there. I sort of didn't want to come back home," she admitted. "But I didn't have anywhere else to go, and it was time, whether I liked it or not."

"Why didn't you want to come home?"

"I lived at colleges for years and then ashrams. The idea of returning to live with my parents wasn't appealing. No independence." She raised one shoulder slightly to suggest her reasoning was to be understood.

"I get that."

"And now I'm living with my parents." Angie stuffed a mouthful of salad into her mouth and rolled her eyes.

Brian put his fork down and looked at her. "So, what's your plan for the future?"

"I have no plan."

"You want to work at a burger joint for the rest of your life?" he joked.

"No, not really," she said laughing and making a face because she didn't like saying that to him.

"Me either and I own the place." Brian laughed as well.

"So, you have bigger plans than owning your own business?"

"I like owning my own business. It has its perks. I just don't want to be flipping burgers when I'm sixty." He picked up his knife and fork again and began cutting the meat on his plate.

"Then what do you want to do?"

"I have no clue."

"I hear you."

For a few moments they sat in silence as they ate. Then Angie broke the silence. "What about your family?"

"My family?" Brian smiled in response. "Good people. The best. My mom works in the school system as a teacher. My dad, well, he's special."

"How so?"

"He's a preacher; very dedicated to his flock, to the Lord. A great man, my role model," he said, nodding. "I had the best parents growing up."

"Do you have siblings?"

"No. I'm an only child."

"Me, too." She smiled at Brian. "Do your folks live around here?"

"Yes, just off Dunlawton in Port Orange." He placed his hand on her shoulder. "We'll go over sometime soon so you can meet them. They'll love you."

"That sounds nice." They had a lot in common. And she felt comfortable being with Brian. That was important. She had a protective father who had instilled in her the desire to continue feeling protected by a male. To feel loved and cared for. She looked to her side at the man next to her as she forked in a chunk of meat and thought, *he's a keeper.*

TWENTY-SEVEN

"WHAT ARE your plans for the day?" Rachel asked.

"I'm caught up on maintenance here, so I thought I'd spend the day at the B and B," Joe said, taking a spoonful of cereal into his mouth.

"Oh, good. Don't forget to take a sandwich with you." Rachel sat back and sipped coffee. It was too early for breakfast, as far as she was concerned. "How did last night go?" She turned her attention toward Angie.

"Great," she said, between bites of toast. Unlike her mother, Angie loved breakfast, especially peanut butter spread on toast. "This man can *cook*."

"You were going to have steak?" Joe asked.

"Yes, and it was perfectly cooked," she answered. "And no ketchup to be had. He doesn't allow anyone to put ketchup on his delectable steaks."

Rachel chuckled. "A man after my heart."

"You should see his cottage. Gorgeous! And it's on the beach," Angie said. "We ate at a picnic table outside, just feet from the ocean. Pure heaven."

"That sounds good. He owns his own place, has his own

business. Impressive." Joe looked up from his cereal. "But is he nice?"

"Oh, Daddy! Such a worry wart. Yes, he's very nice, and an only child," she said, crunching her toast. "His father is a preacher."

"What does the mother do?" Rachel asked.

"She's a teacher. He says he had a great childhood. A lot of people can't say that," Angie said, picking up her coffee. "We have a lot in common, I think."

"It all sounds much better than Josh." Joe gave his daughter the 'eye.' It was the look he wore when he was making a point that she had messed up in some way.

"Yes, from what I can see so far, he is nothing like Josh."

"Did you tell the detective what we found online about Josh and his father?" Rachel asked.

"Yes, I did. And they knew most of it. They're working on the case," Angie said, "but so far Josh hasn't been arrested, only questioned."

"I'd like to see that guy behind bars," Joe said, rising from the table. "He's no good, just trouble."

"And dangerous," Rachel chimed in. "Just like his father."

"What in blue blazes is wrong with people?" Bonnie broke off her rant and started mumbling under her breath as she carried in a bin full of dirty dishes from the dining area.

"What's wrong?" Brian asked, standing back from the griddle.

"Dumb customer. Rude. Like I wasn't busy?" she said, banging the bin onto the counter.

"What do you need?" he asked.

"Apparently I need another arm," she said with exasperation written all over her face.

"Let me have the dishes," he said, sliding the bin to himself. "Take care of the customer."

Bonnie returned immediately to the dining area. The other side of the swinging door opened seconds later. Angie breezed in.

"It's crazy out there," she said. "Total chaos. You need to hire another girl."

"Dee is due in any time," he answered.

"Can't be soon enough," Angie said, collecting clean dishes on a tray and returning to the room of chaos.

Angie was a hard worker, despite her lack of jobs on a resume. She also spoke her mind, which Brian found appealing. That wasn't the only thing about her that was appealing. She could be witty. She could be innocent. She could have a temper flare up, and then flip into an agreeable mood in an instant. She also could be so sweet. And then there was her pretty face. Her face. Brian dreamed about her face the night before. All night. Her beautiful blue eyes glowed when she looked at him. Angie was amazing in Brian's eyes.

A few months ago, he had carried forty extra pounds on his large frame. His mindless eating, mostly out of boredom, had been his undoing. But once Angie came to work for him, he had an incentive to lose the extra pounds. He'd even been lifting weights to help the number on the scale steadily drop lower. Why he hadn't been using them all along, he didn't know. His weights were conveniently parked in the garage, just waiting for him to pay attention. But now he had a desire to get healthy. And her name was Angie.

Dee Tremaine busted through the swinging door, breaking into Brian's thoughts. "Yikes, it's a zoo out there," she said. "You can thank me for being here, Mr. Forbes."

"Now it's Mr. Forbes?"

Dee laughed. "Aren't you old enough to be my daddy?"

"You better be kidding, Miss Tremaine," he joked. "You're not hardly younger than me."

Dee tied her apron around her waist, covering over the pink uniform. "Okay, boss, I'm on the floor." Dee swung out, into the dining area.

Angie sighed as she loaded dirty dishes into a bin. When she turned around, she saw Josh sitting at the edge of a booth next to her. He reached out and took her wrist. "Sit."

"I can't sit, I'm busy. Can't you see how crazy this place is?" She looked at Josh like he'd lost his mind.

Angie tried to move away, but Josh held tight to her wrist. "I said sit, and I mean it."

The expression on his face was dark. Fear shot through Angie like a dose of medicine. She edged the bin onto the table and sat across from him. "What do you want?"

"I want you to stop disrespecting me. Go to the police and tell them you made a mistake about me," he said in a low voice. Although low in volume, she couldn't miss hearing the intimidation. "Tell them anything you can dream up, but make sure they understand that you screwed up. You got it wrong."

"I can't do that," she said. "They'd think I was a goofy girl who didn't know her own mind. Besides, I'd be lying. I don't lie."

Josh leaned closer to her, as he had the last time they had gone out to dinner. She could feel his heat, his anger, it was so potent. And then he spoke. "You will do as you're told or I will make you sorry you ever breathed a word of disrespect about me, Miss Pretty Face."

Her face? A chill shot up her spine, landing in her head. She felt faint, off balance. *My face?*

"Get up!" Brian said, grabbing Josh by the back of his

collar, physically raising the man out of the seat, and dragging him into the aisle. "Don't you ever talk to Angie again, in here or elsewhere. Get out and don't even think about returning." Brian was looking down into the man's face, too close for comfort, with an expression suggesting he meant business. Angie had never seen this side of Brian. "If I see you around here, you're dead meat. I ain't playin'."

When Brian released the collar, Angie noticed Josh's eyes were big. He pulled his black shirt in place, looking a bit shook up. Without saying a word, Josh turned to leave.

"Don't come back," Brian called out as the man exited.

"How did you know?" Angie asked.

"I saw him through the pass-through when he came in. It was obvious he was looking for trouble. Then I knew who he was when I saw you sit with him. Like a flash, it hit me." Brian looked down at Angie. "When I came out and saw your face, there was no doubt."

"Thank you," she said, rising and flinging her arms around him.

"Wow, is this what I have to do to get a hug?" he joked.

Angie leaned back and smiled. "No, I have plenty more."

The customers broke out in applause. Someone called out 'hero.' Brian just laughed.

TWENTY-EIGHT

"Y'ALL, I am so bummed tonight," LuAnn said. She didn't look bummed. Quite the contrary. Dressed in a snazzy red top with sequins dotting various areas, she looked like the Queen of Country Music. Her long red nails flashed in the air as she spoke with her hands. The black jeans she wore flattered every one of her curves. Bummed? Maybe she was seeking attention?

"What's wrong now?" Olivia asked. She eyed LuAnn while swirling a straw in her iced tea. "You look great, girl."

"Derks is definitely going on that tour around the country. And I'm gonna be left here by myself," she said, pouting her full red lips.

"Then go with him," Rachel said.

"I don't want to."

"Go. The building is safe, so you don't need to worry about burglars. And we'll be here when you get back. We aren't going anywhere." Rachel gave her friend an encouraging smile.

LuAnn threw her big blue eyes on her friend. "I don't want to go, Rachel. No desire whatsoever. None. Nada. Zip."

"Tell us how you really feel," Olivia joked.

Trying to change the subject to take LuAnn's mind off Derks, Rachel asked her friend a question. "Tell me something. Do your toes match your fingernails? Are they bright, sparkly red, too?"

LuAnn shot her a peculiar look. "Well, since you asked, the answer is no, honey. My toes are so gnarly, I hide them under cute boots." She stuck out one foot from under the table, revealing fringed black cowgirl boots.

"So I see," Rachel said.

Laughter boomed from the far corner of the Clubhouse where four men were located around the table. They appeared to be playing a card game. Rachel tried to be casual as she looked over at them. She didn't want to appear like she was spying on them, even though she was.

"Those guys are playing cards," LuAnn stated the obvious. "I wonder if they're gambling?"

"Looks like they might be," Rachel said.

"I think that's exactly what they're doing," Olivia chimed in. "From where I'm sitting, I can see bills in the center of the table."

"That's not change from their drinks." Rachel scowled. "Does anyone know those guys?"

Both women said no.

Just as Rachel was about to approach the table, all four men stood and walked out. "I wonder where they're going?"

"One of us needs to trail them," LuAnn said.

"Not you. They can't help but notice you lagging behind," Rachel said.

"So? I can ride the elevator with them; see what floor they get off at." LuAnn stood quickly. "I better hustle or I'll miss them." With long strides of her cowgirl boots, she took off after the men.

Rachel and Olivia looked at each other in silence.

The elevator doors were beginning to close as LuAnn rounded the corner. "Oh, please hold the elevator," she called out in her deepest southern accent. One of the men looked out to see who had spoken and saw LuAnn, hustling toward the elevator. He held the door for her. Of course.

"Oh, thank you, sirs." She sashayed into the elevator with a big smile on her face. "So kind of you to wait for me."

"Our pleasure," one of the men said. "What floor?"

"Eight."

"Already got it punched," he said. "You live here or are you coming to the party?"

"I live here. But tell me about the party," she said, batting her false eyelashes like she was shooing a fly.

"Down in 810, bunch of us are playing poker. High stakes."

"What he means is, you have to pay to get in and guarantee fifty thousand," said another man. "You should come. At least hang out to give us good luck."

"Oh, honey, I don't know anything about poker," LuAnn said, giving the men a coy expression. "And I doubt I'd bring you luck. I've never won anything in my life." She let out a peal of laughter for good measure.

The doors opened and LuAnn stepped out first. She turned around as they exited. "You boys have a good time tonight."

They thanked her and watched her walk away before they turned in the opposite direction. LuAnn stopped and turned around to observe the men. She watched them enter 810 as a woman passed them in the doorway. She was a buxom brunette dressed in a blue dress with a plunging neckline. After she lit a cigarette, she leaned over the railing while she smoked. A different man from the four joined her on the walkway soon after, also lighting up a cigarette.

"Rachel isn't going to like this," she whispered to herself

as she walked back to the elevators. When the doors opened, three more men were inside. LuAnn nodded and gave a slight smile. She waited to the side until they exited and then watched to see where they went. After greeting the couple on the walkway, she saw them enter the unit.

"So, what happened?" Rachel asked as LuAnn returned to the table.

"It's all bad," she said, sitting back in her chair. "I was friendly with the men, so they invited me to a poker game in 810, a high stakes game, they said. A guarantee of fifty thousand and a fee to get in."

"What?" Rachel's eyes were almost bugging out of her face.

"I saw a bimbo with a low-cut dress smoking outside, and then another man, not one of the four, came out to smoke with her. Then when I was getting back on the elevator, three more men were getting out and went into 810. They knew the couple smoking."

Rachel was so angry, she couldn't speak. She kept slapping the armrest with her hands in frustration and looking back and forth from one friend to the other.

"I think she's upset," Olivia said, but not jokingly. "Calm down. This isn't good for your blood pressure or your diabetes, sweetie."

"Ah-h-h-h!" She let out an exasperated sound. "Not – only – is – it – against – the – rules – to – smoke – on – the – walkway," she sputtered, "but it's against the law to – to -- gamble on – the -- the premises."

"Not to mention, gambling without a license," LuAnn said.

"Yes!"

"What are you going to do?" Olivia asked.

"I don't know. I don't think calling the cops will help," she said. "They'll just get off like before. But I will talk to the president of the board -- first thing in the morning. He had something to do with the Brighams buying their unit. He needs to know what's going on. And he can clean up this mess. I don't need to be involved."

The next morning, before Rachel had time to put in a call to Charles Amos, Penelope entered her office. Alfred trailed behind her.

"Morning, Rachel," Alfred said. It was unusual for him to be so bold, speaking before Penelope barely had time to sit in the guest chair.

"Good morning, both of you. What brings you here so early?"

"We need your services as a notary again," Alfred said.

"Yes, please." Penelope smiled at Rachel. Something was off, but she didn't know what.

"What can I do for you?" She looked from one to the other, not sure who would speak.

"Well, uh, we want you to, uh…" Alfred started to say.

"Oh, spit it out, Alfred, for heaven's sake," Penelope said, her face quickly going from a smile to a frown.

Rachel focused on Alfred's face and waited.

"Will you marry us?"

Since Rachel was standing, she felt the need to sit, so she did. "Marry? You want me to marry you two?"

"Yes," Penelope said, smiling again. "Out by the garden. It's a lovely place for a wedding."

Rachel was stupefied. And amused. And feeling a little sentimental. How sweet was this? Two seniors wanting to get married.

"Of course, I'd be delighted to do the honors," Rachel said, smiling at the couple. "When do you want to do it?"

"Saturday. At noon," Penelope said. "In the garden." Evidently Alfred's part had ended, and Penelope took over.

"Wherever you wish, Penelope."

"Nothing fancy. The garden will provide the ambience."

"Yes, it will. Do you have your dress?"

"Yes. Something I had tucked in the back of the closet for this occasion."

"O-oh," Rachel said, making the word slide into two syllables. Her head swirled with questions she could not ask. How long had she been planning this wedding? How old was this dress? Was it white? Had Penelope been saving it for years until her true love came upon the scene? And then the thought struck Rachel: in what condition is this dress?

"I can't wait to see the dress you chose," Rachel said, nodding her head.

"Me, too," piped up Alfred.

TWENTY-NINE

RACHEL'S next act of business was to call Charles Amos, the president of the residents' association for the condo. He picked up on the second ring.

"Charles, it's Rachel," she said after she heard his raspy voice. "I need to talk to you, so I hope this is a good time."

"Do you want me to come down to your office?"

"Yes, that would be a good idea. This is important."

"On my way now." Charles hung up the phone.

Five minutes later, Charles walked into her office. He was a skinny man with a shock of white hair bushing out from his head, giving him a top-heavy appearance. His eyebrows were unusually bushy as well, and he sported an equally plush white mustache. He didn't hesitate to sit in the guest chair across from Rachel.

"What's so important?" he asked, crossing his lanky legs.

"There was a poker game last night in 810. That's the Brigham's unit, in case you don't remember." Rachel sat back in her chair, resting her elbows on the armrests, and joining her hands in front. She waited to see how he reacted to this announcement.

"So? A friendly game of poker, that's no big deal." Charles crossed his arms across his chest. "Perfectly fine entertainment."

"It may have been friendly and entertaining, as you say, but it was illegal." Rachel didn't let her gaze waver.

Charles uncrossed and re-crossed his legs to the other side. "Nah, not in a private home. No way."

"Charles," she said, glancing down briefly, "it is illegal to charge an entry fee and conduct a high stakes game with a minimum of $50,000 required to get into the game. Not to mention, these weren't people from our condo. They were outsiders, coming to a poker game that the Brighams were offering. This is not a gambling establishment. It's a residential condominium that caters to the fifty plus crowd."

"So, what's the harm? Nobody got killed. Nobody got shot," he said, laughing off her comments. "You're just being silly."

What was it with the men lately calling women silly? She didn't appreciate the term; it was demeaning.

"The harm? It was illegal, Charles!" She leaned forward with her arms placed on her desk. "There were a lot of people present. Mostly men, with a sprinkling of dressed up women to keep them company, is my guess. This was not a friendly game of poker. The Brighams put on an illegal gaming event."

"May I remind you that gambling is legal in Florida," he said between gritted teeth. Rachel could see that he was angry.

"It is not legal unless you have a license and are running a gaming establishment. The condo is not a gaming establishment, Mr. President," she said with all the firmness she could muster. "I know this is awkward, especially since you were at the game last night." She didn't know that for sure, only had suspicions, but it was worth a shot to see his reaction.

"Me? Why would you say that?" His expression changed immediately. His face morphed into a little boy innocent look.

"You were seen, Charles. No one who lives here looks quite like you, and I doubt much of anybody else in Daytona Beach."

The man's mouth tightened. She had him.

"Look," he said, uncrossing his legs, leaning forward, and placing his elbows on his knees. "I've lived here a long time. Maybe too long. There's not much to do here, except swim. Or maybe go down to the clubhouse. We need some diversion, some entertainment, you know? A little game of poker, what can it harm?"

"How many times do I have to say it's illegal?" Rachel looked him square in the eyes. "You know it is. And you knew who you were allowing to buy a unit when you gave the thumbs up for John Brigham. That's why he and his son were given special consideration. I wasn't born yesterday, Charles. Don't you go to Vegas frequently?"

He sat back in his chair with a sigh. He was caught and he knew it. "What do you want me to do about it?"

"Get rid of them."

"It's not that easy. John owns the unit. We can't just evict him like a renter."

"Then figure it out. Make life uncomfortable for them. Take a trip to our attorney and ask about having them removed," she suggested, grabbing a pen in her hand, and pointing it at him. "And tell your buddy, John, not to hold any more games."

Charles' eyes grew big and his lips flapped a bit before he spoke. "M-me? I can't do that. I'll talk to the attorney, anything else you think would help – but I'm not talking to him." The man was seriously rattled by the idea of any discussion about discontinuing the poker games. Obviously, he knew John Brigham was not a man to mess with.

"Okay, then go into action. Make an appointment to see the attorney." Rachel felt she had won the debate.

"Right on it, Rachel," he said, rising. Rachel thought she saw his hands shaking. "I'll be in touch."

"Please do."

Rachel broke out her fan after he left and began waving air on herself. *That went pretty well.*

LuAnn set her drink back on the table and drummed her long nails on the side of the glass as she waited for Olivia and Rachel. The two women walked in together, having met in the elevator. "There's our girl," Olivia said as she sat in one of the chairs. She was smiling and happy looking in her free time clothing of jeans and a sweater.

"You been here long?" Rachel asked, sitting in between the two women. She raised her arm and the server scurried over. "I want iced tea. I think she does as well."

"Yes, iced tea, please," Olivia said.

"Not too long. I'm just relaxing." LuAnn had a more casual appearance that evening. Her hair was pulled straight back into a ponytail, which was highly unusual. Normally she had her hair pouffed out or piled high on her head. And the jeans she wore were baggy, with a slouchy blue top falling over.

"You look comfy," Rachel said. She hadn't had time to change from her office clothes.

"You look fantastic," Olivia said to Rachel. Her white shirt still looked crisp over her black dress slacks.

"Well, thank you. I'm feeling better now by eating right

and taking my meds. The diabetes numbers have been within a good range, I'm happy to say."

"I'm just chilling out." LuAnn did a casual flip of her ponytail with one hand. "No reason to get all dolled up."

"You haven't found a gig?" Rachel asked.

"Nope. Nothing. In a couple weeks, no problem, just not anything currently available."

"So, Derks left to go on the road?" Olivia asked, accepting her drink from the server.

"Yes, unfortunately. I couldn't get him to stay local since the other guys wanted to do the road gig." LuAnn sighed, then lifted her glass to her lips, sans lipstick. "I suggested we do a duo, but he's really got the itch to experience the road."

"He'll find out it's not what it's cracked up to be," Rachel said, accepting her iced tea.

"But at what cost? Will he still be my man when he returns? Will the drooling females pump his ego so much he thinks he's the next Tim McGraw?" When she plunked her glass down, it made a loud thud that emphasize her dismay.

Rachel looked over at her friend with concern stamped on her face. "You don't know, he could be turned off by the hype and superficiality."

LuAnn swung her head toward Rachel. "Right. First time on the road? Not likely. He'll eat it up."

Rachel decided to change the subject. "I had a talk with Charles about the gambling activity at the Brigham's unit."

"Ooh, what did he say?" Olivia asked.

"At first, he defended them, saying it was legal. Really?" Rachel rolled her eyes. "Then he had to admit he was at the game when I said he was seen there."

"He was there?" Olivia asked.

"Yes. I didn't know for sure, but I sort of tricked him." Rachel couldn't help but grin at her cleverness. "You see, I thought the sale to them was odd, and it was sort of a wink and a nod arrangement because of the preferential treatment given to them. It's obvious to me that Charles knew about the gambling before they moved in."

"Doesn't Charles go to Vegas a lot?" Olivia asked.

"He sure does, which added to my suspicions. So, I told him to talk to John."

"What did he say to that?" LuAnn asked.

"He refused, which I can't blame him. Then he agreed to talk to our attorney and work on some way to get him out." She took a few sips of her drink and leaned against the chair back, drink still in hand. "This is a mess. Can you imagine, running a poker game out of one of our units? Add onto that, John and Josh are dangerous. Sickening. I'm afraid to live in my condo."

"Have you been threatened since the last time John came into your office?" Olivia asked.

"No, not me, but Angie was. She told us about Josh coming into the diner where she works and how he threatened her." Rachel looked down while trying to collect herself. "He told her to tell the police she got it wrong, that she made a mistake. She refused and he told her, in so many words, he'd mess up her face if she didn't."

"Her face? What did she do?" LuAnn asked.

"Well, fortunately, Brian, you know, the guy who owns the place? He stepped in and yanked Josh out of the booth and told him never to come back. You haven't met Brian, but he's a big guy and Josh, although a nasty cuss, isn't that big."

"So, what did Josh do?" Olivia asked.

"Nothing. Angie said he looked rattled. He just walked out without saying anything."

"Good for Brian, Angie's hero," LuAnn said.

"It's a little more than that," Rachel said, smiling slightly. "They are seeing each other."

"Oh, how sweet," Olivia said, always the romantic.

"He has a nice cottage on the beach, paid for, no less. Obviously, he owns his business. He's doing well for himself." Rachel looked happy for her daughter.

Olivia clasped her hands together. "I'm so happy for her."

"Me, too," LuAnn said.

"Me three." Rachel took a sip of her tea.

THIRTY

SATURDAY ROLLED AROUND, and Rachel was admittedly excited at the prospect of uniting the elder couple in matrimony. She loved weddings. They always left her feeling romantic for days after. As she stood looking into her closet, she remembered her own wedding. It had been quirky and fun. But that reminiscing would have to wait for another time. Today she had to figure out what to wear to this one.

"What time is the wedding?" Joe asked as he stepped from the bathroom, having just finished his shower.

"Noon. In the garden."

"I can dress casual?"

"Sure, you're not in the wedding party." She kept sliding hangers over until she found the perfect dress, the pink one. It was tailored, clean lines, and cool enough for the noon sun. She also had pink heels that matched the dress perfectly. That's why she bought them. Any excuse to buy shoes was a good excuse.

She put on the dress and shoes, then added appropriate jewelry to compliment her outfit. She liked what she saw in the mirror, despite the tummy she had gained in the last year.

It didn't protrude too much in this dress, fortunately. She knew this came as a result of her change of life. While her waistline had become more defined, her behind had flattened and all that fat had seemed to move around to the front. Voila – a tummy was born.

Rachel gathered her paperwork and was ready to leave. "Joe, I'm ready to go."

"Right behind you." He joined her by the door, dressed in simple slacks and a sports shirt. He was dressy casual, for Florida, anyway.

They arrived at the garden and Rachel picked the logical spot for her to stand and deliver the wedding vows. Two aisles wove around and through the center of the garden, allowing for the groom to walk down one side and the bride the other, plus any attendants who might participate. As she stood looking out, she had to agree this was perfect for a wedding because of the ocean sliding into the sand some yards behind the garden where she would stand. Daytona perfection.

A woman she did not recognize with bright red hair that could compete with Ruby's color hustled over to her. She was a little heavy and definitely breathless when she reached Rachel. "Hi, I'm Margaret," she said, extending her hand. "I'm Alfred's daughter."

"Oh, so nice to meet you," Rachel said. "I'm Rachel. It's nice you're here to support your father."

The woman laughed, her body heaving some. "Yeah, well, crazy old geezer. Who gets married at his age?"

"Probably not many people. But then, not many live to be his age."

"That is true. My husband is out there somewhere," she said swinging her arm behind. "I don't think my brothers could make it. One I know didn't want to come. Thought Dad was off his rocker." Again, she laughed.

"Have you met the bride?"

"No. Is she nice?"

"She's sweet, most times, a little bossy, and a bit religious. I would describe her as proper." *To say the least.*

"Hmm. Whatever, I'm not marrying her. Ha!" Margaret laughed again.

Some of the residents began to gather. Several were using walkers, two were in wheelchairs, and the rest she guessed would have to stand. There was no seating in the garden, except for the one cement bench.

A boy Rachel guessed to be about eleven, appeared. "Hey, I'm Timmy. I'm the grandson."

"Nice to meet you, Timmy," she said, taking the hand he offered.

"I'm in charge of the music." He was short for his age, wore big brown glasses over his eyes and a ready smile. Dressed in a child's suit, he was adorable.

"Really? That's very nice of you to do."

"Yeah, I got this device. It will fill the area with sound." He held it up in the air.

Rachel had never seen anything quite like the electronic device he held in his hand. It wasn't very large, but then, electronics were incredibly small nowadays. "Is that your mom?" She pointed toward Margaret.

"No. She's over there." Timmy pointed at another woman who was just entering the garden. The woman had similar features to Margaret but was much slimmer. Her hair was a natural brown, and she wore a simple printed dress sufficient to tolerate the heat of the day.

A man approached Rachel whom she figured was one of the two women's husbands. He was tall and a nice weight. She thought he belonged to the daughter she hadn't met yet.

"Penelope wanted me to tell you that she's standing at the door with my father-in-law."

"Okay, thank you. Then we'll begin." No one had shared any information about the proceedings, so Rachel was winging the ceremony, waiting for instruction. She looked over at Timmy and pointed at him to start the music. And the music began.

Penelope and Alfred walked out the door that opened onto a cement path that led to the garden. The instrumental version of *I'll Be Loving You, Always* wafted through the air as they walked. Penelope held Alfred's arm while carrying a small bouquet of white roses in her other hand as they made their slow procession over to the garden. Everyone was standing in anticipation, except the few in wheelchairs. Once inside the garden, Alfred walked on the left side while Penelope walked down the right side of the path that was divided by beautiful flowering bushes. Red roses bloomed to the right of Penelope and yellow mums flourished to the left of Alfred. He was dressed in a soft gray suit as he slowly made his way down the aisle. But the bride! She stole the show.

Penelope wore a full-length white dress, complete with a simple veil that fell to the middle of her back. The dress had full, plain sleeves that draped to her wrists and were tucked into a cuff. The bodice hugged her body and was covered in pearls. The high lace neck snuggly crept up to her chin, while the skirt below billowed in the sea breeze. Rachel thought the dress was stunning, not to mention highly unique for a woman her age to wear. She guessed that dress had been hanging in Penelope's closet for decades, expertly cared for to be in such pristine condition. Beneath her dress, as Penelope walked, Rachel noticed the toes of her white sneakers peeking out.

Once they reached the place where Rachel was standing, she motioned for Timmy to turn off the music and whispered to the couple where to stand. She began the ceremony, feeling grateful that she had chosen very traditional vows for the elder couple. When it came to the part where they were to exchange rings, a man and a woman jumped up from the cement bench to participate, each standing in the appropriate spot. Penelope handed her bouquet to the woman, who Rachel did not recognize. She delivered the vows, and the couple individually recited them after her. The man produced the ring for Penelope at the appropriate time, and the woman did the same with Alfred's ring.

"I now pronounce you husband and wife. You may kiss your bride."

Alfred didn't miss a beat. He planted a solid kiss on Penelope's lips, then smiled broadly. Everyone applauded the happy couple as they turned to face the gathering before them.

Rachel took in an emotional breath and fought back tears of joy, remembering her wedding day vividly. She could only hope that Alfred and Penelope would be as happy as she and Joe had been, for whatever time they had left together.

THIRTY-ONE

A WEEK LATER, Charles abruptly walked into Rachel's office. He had not made an appointment, as was his custom, so she was surprised to see him.

"Hello, Charles."

"Yeah, Rachel, good morning." He plopped into the chair, his bony legs sticking from under his blue shorts. "I just left the attorney's office."

"Oh, good. What did he say?" She put the pen in her hand on the desk and listened attentively.

"The attorney's suggestion is for him to send a certified letter to John Brigham demanding he never hold a poker game, or any other sort of gambling, in his residence. He said the letter he composed would say if such activity continued, the condo association would seek relief, which could mean him being removed from the building."

"That's fair. It also takes the weight off of you and me for making the demand," she said, easing back into her chair. "And it meets our objective. No gambling. Of course, they still live here, but at least it avoids the messiness of removing them."

"As long as they don't hold another game," Charles said, leaning back in his chair, too. "Then we'd have another situation to deal with."

"I don't think he'll hold another game, Charles," she said, looking satisfied with the proposed solution. "Not to say he's learned a lesson, but we could have been much tougher on him, maybe got the cops involved."

"I agree with you."

"If he wants to have other games in the town where he lives, there are plenty of places to choose from. And there are other cities and states he can go to without affecting his residence." Rachel smiled at the older man.

"You're right. Lots of other places, just not here," Charles said, smiling back.

"You did good, Charles."

"I did what was right, that's all. And I apologize for my wrong thinking and subsequent behavior," he said, looking down and shaking his head. "What an idiot I was to turn my back on the rules and the law. I don't know what got into me. I am truly sorry, Rachel." He looked straight into her face when he said those words.

"It's okay. You cleaned up your mess. Now, if John just keeps himself clean up there on the eighth floor, all will be fine." Rachel felt relief and satisfaction over Charles' news and repentant attitude. Things were turning around. Yes, indeed.

"Oh, I am so proud of you," Rachel said, her face beaming at her husband.

"Yeah, I finished up in record time," Joe said.

The couple lounged on the comfy chairs on the balcony, discussing recent events at the end of the week. For one, the finalizing of the renovation of the B and B Joe had been diligently working on.

"It's actually ready to rent," Rachel mused.

"Yes. We just have to market it."

"Who's going to do that?" she asked. Neither one of them was schooled in marketing or had enough knowledge of the Internet to be proficient in showcasing the B and B.

"I was thinking of Angie," Joe said.

Rachel sat up in her chair, looking at her husband. "Joe, that's brilliant! Doesn't she have a degree in marketing? We could give her a cut of each rental for her work."

"Exactly what I was thinking," Joe said. "Maybe she can eventually work her way out of that diner."

"Except she's dating the owner, you will remember. Maybe she doesn't want to leave."

"Hmm. Well, we can ask."

It wasn't long after their conversation that Angie came home. Rachel was in the kitchen fixing dinner, Joe setting the table.

"Hey, Angie," Joe said, looking up from the table as he placed the utensils around the plates. "Your mother and I have something to ask you."

"Sure, what?" she walked into the kitchen and gave her mother a kiss on the cheek as she stood in front of the counter.

Joe walked over to the kitchen, leaning on the door jamb. "The B and B is finished and ready to be marketed."

"That's fantastic, Daddy."

"And we thought you would be the perfect person to do the marketing. If you're interested."

Angie's eyes grew bigger. "Wow, what a surprise. I do have a degree in marketing."

"That's what I thought," Rachel interjected.

"And we would pay you to market our property," Joe said.

"This isn't a freebee we expect. You would earn a percentage of the rentals."

"Yeah, that sounds fair," she said as she considered the offer.

Rachel threw out a thought, seeing if it stuck or not. "We also thought you might, eventually, be able to break away from working at the diner. That is, if you wanted to."

"Well, we all know I'm an overeducated server. Working there is ridiculous. And Brian would understand," she said, nodding.

"You don't have to give us an answer right now," Joe said. "You can think about it and let us know."

"No, I don't need to think about it. I'll take the job," she said firmly. "I can use it to propel me into the marketing world. Gain experience in the field and so forth."

Rachel and Joe looked at their daughter with curiosity.

"You want to enter marketing?" Joe asked.

"Not until you offered me this opportunity. It sounds like a good idea; just what I need to get me started in a direction for my future. Thanks, guys," she said, hugging her mother first and then her father. "I didn't know where I was going until right now. I always liked marketing and I excelled in the classes. So, why not do marketing?"

"Oh, Angie, I'm so happy for you," Rachel said.

"Me, too, pumpkin," said a proud father. "You could consider living in one of the bedrooms, if you want some independence."

"Hmm, that sounds good. Except, it would take away the rental profit of that bedroom," Angie said, walking toward the dining room table with a casserole in her hands. "Maybe after a while of renting them out and I get a good job in marketing, I could move into a bedroom."

"Whatever you think is wise, sweetheart," Rachel said.

"Yes, whatever you want to do, it's okay by us. Just one

thing I ask: take Precious with you." They laughed at that remark while Precious and Benny were eye to eye in the living room, having a discussion. A loud one.

Everyone sat at the table. "May I say grace tonight?" Angie asked.

"Sure," Joe said.

"Thank you, Father, for this wonderful day and my awesome parents who have just blessed me with an opportunity for my future. We ask blessings upon this food for the nourishment of our bodies." All said amen.

From Rachel's position behind the large windows in her office, she saw John and Josh enter the elevator cubicle. They were holding one singular envelope, which she figured was the certified letter from the attorney. She knew the mail had already come, so they would have had to go to the post office to claim it after they received the notification card in the mailbox. John opened the letter as they waited for the elevator, while Josh looked on with interest. They shared a few words as John was reading the contents. Josh looked over toward the office, as if he suspected she had something to do with the letter from an attorney. He couldn't see her looking at him because of the way she had her head positioned downward with her eyes looking out the corners. Neither appeared angry when the elevator door opened, and they got in.

Now they knew. Now they also knew *she* knew, and that potentially Charles was involved. But the attorney wrote the letter, not either one of them. Hopefully, they accepted the news from the attorney and saw it as removed from management's decision. Hopefully.

THIRTY-TWO

THEY WERE the only two left at the diner as they finished cleaning up the grease from the grill, griddle, and stove.

"Brian," she said softly, "I have some news."

"What's that?" he asked as he scraped the griddle.

"I told you about my parents buying a house and that my dad was going to remodel it to be a B and B."

"Yes, you did."

"Well, Daddy finished the renovation and it's ready to market for rentals." She stopped wiping the stove and turned toward him. "They want me to market it to the public. I would get a percentage of the rental price. And if I want, I can move into the house and live in one of the bedrooms."

"That sounds awesome, Angie." He stopped what he was doing and looked at her. "You're going to do it, aren't you?"

"Yes. I don't think I'll move in yet, not until I get some experience and then seek a real job in marketing." She waited to hear his reply.

"Angie, it sounds like you have finally figured out what you want to do with your life," he said with sincerity beaming from his eyes.

"Yes, it does, doesn't it?" She laughed softly. "I think I have. I really liked marketing in college. And with the experience I get at the B and B, I can eventually walk into a job interview with credentials and capability."

Brian walked over to where she stood leaning against the stove. He reached out to hold her in his arms. "I'm proud of you," he said, planting a kiss on her cheek. "But you're staying here for a while yet?"

"Oh, sure. I need to gain the experience of marketing the B and B and get the rentals coming in before I apply for a job with a company."

"How do you plan to work here and do all that?"

"Get up earlier?" She laughed as she looked into his face.

"How about you work one less day here. At first. If you need more time, then I'll arrange for coverage through Bonnie and Dee, and hire another girl part time." He looked down at her pretty face aglow with happiness.

"That sounds wonderful, Brian. Thank you," she said, standing on tiptoes to kiss his cheek.

"Eventually, when you get that job with a company, I'll hire someone to take your position, but not your place," he said. "No one can replace you." This time he kissed her on the lips.

Only recently did she know what it meant to have sparks fly. It took until she was twenty-five to feel the electricity she had only heard or read about. She realized that she was different from the other girls she worked with. They were more experienced in life and romance, but she had chosen a different path a long time ago. Maybe that was why she lingered in college and then lived in ashrams? Not that college wasn't full of temptations. Everything imaginable had paraded by to tempt her values, but she stuck to what she believed. She wasn't popular in college as a result, but that was okay with her. She was there to get an education, not party or find a husband.

A career was her goal, so she continued earning degrees. Then the dilemma presented itself of what to do with all of them. She had majored in business. There was a degree in marketing, another in finance. As she looked back on her past choices, Angie was feeling fortunate to have chosen a business path. She could open a business, manage a business for someone, or go into marketing. In retrospect, her choices had all been good ones. She felt confident her future would be equally good.

Her love choice with Brian was certainly promising, although she didn't know if they had a permanent connection. Time would tell with that. It was too early in their relationship to determine where their paths would end up, joined or separated. God knew. She trusted God in that department.

"Now it's your turn to find your path," she said, stepping back from the embrace.

"Yeah, whatever that is."

"You'll know when it presents itself. Just like me, right out of the blue, my path was placed in my lap. The questions were answered. You can't force His will." Angie picked up her rag and turned back to cleaning the stove again.

"Look at you, getting all smart on me," Brian said, walking back to the griddle. "I'm proud of you, Angie."

"Thanks. That means a lot."

John and Josh walked into Rachel's office, neither smiling nor looking friendly. Rachel was immediately on guard.

"Rachel," John said, nodding at her. Josh didn't say anything.

"John."

"We came to inform you that there will be no gambling in our unit, not that there was in the first place. That was all a big lie someone made up to hurt us," he said, still standing, with Josh a step behind him.

Rachel didn't believe the man. She believed LuAnn saw what she reported, and that Charles was present at the game and tried to pull a fast one by allowing the Brighams to purchase the unit. All of that she believed, but she wasn't going to argue with the man. Let him suggest his alternative view, it wasn't important what untruth he was trying to convey.

"That would be appreciated, if you didn't offer gambling in your unit ever again."

"Not that we ever did."

"Whatever."

"Now, for that concession, I'm asking something from you." So far, his demeaner was calm. But Rachel couldn't imagine what he wanted.

"Such as?" she asked.

"For your daughter to tell the police that she misunderstood. She got it wrong. Josh didn't have anything to do with the beating of that man," he said. "I think that's a fair deal."

"I don't. Because that would be a lie. Did you teach Josh to lie?" she said, looking for a reaction in his expression. There was none. "Because I didn't teach my daughter to lie and I'm certainly not going to make that suggestion to her now."

John's eyes squinted in response and his face clouded with anger. "You, you don't know what you're saying, lady." Josh took hold of his father's arm, mumbling something into his ear. John wrenched his arm free of the grip. He pointed at Rachel with the same arm. "Better watch out, Mrs. Barnes. Bad things happen to nice people."

He turned abruptly away and walked to the door. Josh

glanced at Rachel as he followed his father out of the office. She had the feeling Josh didn't support his father's statements.

She sat back in her chair, trembling. *Another threat from that awful man. What next?*

Later that night during dinner, Joe was upset over the news his wife conveyed about the encounter with the Brighams. He pushed his plate away in frustration. "I can't believe that man had the nerve to threaten you again – and Angie. What is wrong with those people? Who goes around threatening people like that?"

"Godless people. I'm so concerned about Angie," Rachel said, wiping her lips with a napkin.

"Be concerned for yourself, too."

"I don't know what to do, Joe. Contacting the police is futile at this point."

"We're going to contact them anyway. *If* something happens, there will be no doubt who is behind the action. Let's call right now," he said, pushing away from the table and walking toward the phone. Joe dialed the number he had written on the tablet the last time he spoke to them.

Rachel joined him on the couch, waiting to be connected to the appropriate office. Once Joe was able to reach someone, he spoke briefly to them and then handed the phone to Rachel. She explained the exchange between herself and John Brigham, emphasizing that this was a recurring action toward her and her family. She was told that this information would be added to the previous and assured that the new threat would not go unnoticed.

"Don't worry, I'll protect you," Joe said after she hung up the phone.

"You can't stand guard at my office every day, Joe." She sat on the couch, looking wide eyed and vulnerable.

"No, you're right about that." He swung his arm around her shoulders, the least he could do.

"And Angie can't stay cloistered in our unit. She works." Rachel placed her head on Joe's chest.

"Brian will take care of her at work. I'm not worried about her being there," he said, circling both arms around his wife.

"Me either. Just in between here and there." She looked up at her husband, and the couple stared into each other's eyes, reading their mutual concern for their only child.

THIRTY-THREE

WHEN SUNDAY MORNING CAME, the entire family was assembled at the door to attend church. Each had a particular need to fulfill from within that sanctuary. Never had they encountered such a threat from an outside source wishing to do harm to any one of them. It was beyond comprehension how this menace could verbally attack the women within the family and suggest they may be physically harmed. And so, they prayed.

As soon as they returned from church, feeling at peace and protected, Angie began to prepare for her beach date with Brian. He was bringing the food, so all she had to do was change into a bathing suit, grab her hat and sunscreen to put in her bag, and she'd be ready to go. When the doorbell rang, Angie hustled to the door.

"Hey," she said, after she looked through the peephole and opened the door. A smile greeted Brian.

"Hey, yourself," he said, bending to give her a quick kiss. "You look ready."

"I am." She was wearing her favorite black and white polka-dot bikini and a white coverup.

"Where are your parents?"

"They're out at the pool."

Brian had met her parents several weeks ago when he had come over for dinner for just that purpose. All had gone well, not like in the movie, *Meet the Parents*. Each had later expressed what a wonderful man Brian is and how they heartily approved of their relationship. The young couple had their blessing.

"Well, let's go then."

Brian picked up her bag, Angie grabbed her hat, and they walked out the door. They decided to walk down to a quieter area south of the condo in order to enjoy a different view, selecting a place near the lifeguard stand. A significant number of people were enjoying the warm weather with them.

"The gang didn't mind you taking a Sunday off?" Angie asked. Weekends were the busiest time for people to come into his burger joint. Brian couldn't afford to close on Sundays.

"Nah. The kid I've been training on the grill and griddle, Dan Winebrenner, was excited to work in my place. He's saving for college, so he wants more hours now that he's got the hang of things. And that means I get to spend time with you," he said, straightening the blanket over the sand. "A man's gotta have a day off. Seven days a week is too much of a grind."

Angie sat on the smooth blanket, lifting her face to the sun for a few moments before she plopped on her sunhat and smoothed sunblock on her body, the scent of coconut wafting up. She used to strive to get a nice tan, but now that she was in her mid-twenties, she saw the wisdom in avoiding a tan. She took rigorous care of her skin, always wearing sunblock, especially on her face. Satisfied she had done what she could to avoid burning, she laid on her back.

Brian lowered his muscular frame to the blanket beside Angie. "It's gorgeous today," he said, looking out to the sea rolling onto the shore.

"Yes, it is. We are in heaven," she said, propping herself on her arms to look at the waves gently rolling toward them. "I never liked the humidity of Florida during certain times of the year, but today is a low humidity day, and it's glorious."

"A great day to relax on the beach."

"For sure."

They laid in the sun for some time, with Brian dozing off to sleep eventually. *The poor guy is exhausted. He needs more time off.* Now that Dan is available to step in to cook, Angie thought Brian would take more time to enjoy life. With her. The prospect was exciting.

The smell of the salt air was refreshing to Angie, one of the many perks of coming to the beach. She felt as contented as she had ever felt in her life during one specific moment. Even meditation hadn't made her feel this relaxed or content. Actually, she hadn't thought about this until now, but she hadn't meditated in quite some time. When needing solace and answers, she had turned to the Bible, not the usual meditation of the past. She felt like a prodigal daughter, returning home, literally, and embracing her roots. It was amazing how life could turn around.

The unmistakable rumble of a motorcycle engine jarred her thoughts. A formidable man without a shirt rode his Hog on the packed-down sand in front of her, then turned close by to park behind her. She lifted half her body to watch him. He wore a black bandana around his forehead and ripped black jeans over his legs. The biker bent to remove his boots as he glanced over to see Angie watching him. He threw up one hand in greeting. For a second, Angie wondered if they had met? Working where she did, she came across many people only one time, so she easily forgot their faces.

Instinctively, she raised her hand in response. The man shoved his boots into a carry-all attached to his bike and began walking toward Angie. Her heart jumped in response. She was glad Brian lay next to her, although still asleep.

"Hey," the biker said to her. He was so large and muscular, the sight of him made Angie's throat clutch. She didn't want any trouble from him, so she sneaked her hand toward Brian and flipped the back of it against his bare skin a couple times to wake him.

"Huh?" Brian said, raising his head.

"Hi," the biker said, looking down from his exalted position.

"Hi. Hey, Brian, we have a visitor," she said, smiling a little and sitting fully upright on the blanket.

When Brian saw the visitor, he raised himself into position. "Hey, man."

"Do I know you?" Angie asked after she realized he looked somewhat familiar.

"Angie, right?" he asked.

"Yes."

"You work at Brian's Burgers." It wasn't a question, rather, a statement.

"Yes, and this is Brian himself," she said, indicating with her hand the man beside her.

"Nice to meet you, man," the biker said, extending his hand. "Great burgers. We come in when in town."

"Hey, awesome," Brian said, extending his hand to the man. "Glad you like them."

"Haven't seen you since that night," the biker said, placing both hands on his hips and looking directly at Angie.

"Which night was that?" Angie asked.

"When that dude was harassing you. The older guy." He pulled out a pack of cigarettes from his back pocket as he talked.

"Oh, of course!" Suddenly, Angie knew exactly who this man was. He and another biker had rescued her when James was driving by on the beach, wanting her to get in his car so he could drive her home. "I was so grateful to you two for rescuing me."

Brian looked confused. "What?"

"I told you about two bikers coming to my rescue when James wanted me to get in his car, you know, when I was walking home that night, after work," Angie said, looking at Brian. "Remember? This is one of the guys."

"Oh, yeah. Hey, thanks, man, for doing that," he said, making a fist and tapping his heart with it. "I owe you."

"It's okay, man. She's a good lady. I couldn't let that dude bother her." The biker shifted from one leg to the other as he talked, lighting his cigarette, and taking a drag.

"So, you're early for bike week," Brian said.

"A little. We left before we had planned last time, so we came early this go-round," he said, acting like he had something more to say, but not sure how to say it. "We had to get out of town fast," he said with a wink.

"I understand." Angie really had no way of knowing what he was talking about, she just figured he had a run in with someone or a deal went bust. Whatever, she knew it was illegal. Why else would they feel the need to leave town in a hurry?

"Yeah, he had it coming, bothering you like that. I know the kind. He was dangerous," the biker said, shaking his head side to side, then taking another drag from his cigarette. "If you'd gotten into that car, well…who knows what he would have done to you?"

A sudden pang sliced into her heart. "Yes, I didn't feel good about that situation." Angie choked out her reply as her heart raced. "What was your name?"

"They call me Hawk." He pointed to the arm that sported

a large tattoo of a hawk. "Griffon. But I'm known as Hawk because I like to be free; sail through the air on my Hog."

"I see," she said, smiling at the man. "Well, Hawk, thank you for rescuing me."

"No problem, miss. I kinda enjoyed settling the score for you," he said, giving her a salute as he turned to leave.

"Thanks again," Brian said after the man.

"Brian!" she hissed his name as she turned to him, her voiced lowered. The biker was walking down the beach, probably out of hearing range. "Did you catch what he was saying?"

"I sure did."

"He beat up James, not Josh. It was *him!*" Angie's blue eyes were wide open and sparking with adrenaline.

Brian studied her pretty face, flushed with heat and excitement. "That's what I gathered. You need to call the police."

"Yes, I do." Angie grabbed her phone from the satchel, dialing the 911 number. When someone answered, she explained she knew who had inadvertently killed James Mason, one of their open murder cases. She was quickly passed through to a detective.

"He said his name was Hawk Griffon. Hawk isn't his real name, of course, just his handle. I guess you call it, a handle, right? He's got a hawk tattoo on his left arm, and right now he's shirtless, walking down the beach, south of the lifeguard stand at Silver Beach." Angie rattled off what she remembered quickly. "He's driving a black Hog, but he doesn't live in our area. So, he's on the beach right now, barefoot, wearing a black bandana, ripped black jeans, and no shirt."

Angie listened to the person talking on the other end of the call. "Yes, he parked his bike at the Silver Beach ramp and left just a few minutes ago, walking south." She paused when the other person talked. "I don't know where he's staying, but he referenced 'we' so he's probably staying with other biker types." Again, she paused in her conversation. "Yes, he said the guy had it coming, and he couldn't let him bother me. He admitted that he 'enjoyed settling the score' for me. Those were his words, settling the score. But I don't think he intended to kill him, just beat him up."

She looked at Brian and raised her eyebrows, asking silently if there was more to relay. He shook his head no. She clicked off the phone after giving a more detailed description of the bike, including the license plate number.

"We should leave before he comes back," Brian said, rising and gathering items.

"It wasn't Josh after all." Angie looked up at him.

"Apparently not," Brian said.

"Wait till I tell Mom and Daddy."

THIRTY-FOUR

AFTER LUANN CALLED Rachel and Olivia to meet at the clubhouse, she dressed herself in baggy jeans and a plain shirt. She swept her hair into a ponytail, not bothering to wear makeup, nor take the time to put on earrings. Her anger was mounting as LuAnn stomped out of the unit, her footfalls making plenty of noise that the downstairs neighbor would certainly object to.

As soon as she arrived at the clubhouse, she ordered a draft. Rachel and Olivia appeared almost immediately after.

"Hey, what's up?" Rachel asked as she sat.

"Yes, what's so important to call a meeting?" Olivia pulled out her chair.

"Sit. It's a long tale," LuAnn said. Her expression was one of consternation and annoyance.

When the server arrived with LuAnn's draft, the two women ordered iced teas.

"I've been missing Derks," LuAnn said, taking a sip from her mug. "He's been calling me, real sweet and all, most every night after he gets done the gig. Unless they have to get on the road right after."

Rachel and Olivia nodded in unison.

"So, I knew they were heading to Denver for two nights. I had a thought: pay the dear man a visit," she said, setting the mug on the table. "Surprise your honey; make him remember you so he knows what a special lady he left at home."

"And so, you flew to Denver?" Rachel asked.

"Yes. I got there in time to go backstage before the last set ended. I watched them perform and, I have to admit, they were really good." She paused when the server returned with the iced teas, then continued. "I started feeling bad for objecting to the band traveling. Like, who am I to interfere with their careers? Rachel, Olivia, they were so *good!*" she said, looking from one to the other. "I realized I had been acting like a selfish, spoiled brat to stand in Derks' way. He needs this experience, this success in his life."

"That's big of you to admit, LuAnn," Olivia said, nodding her head. "Good for you."

"Thank you. I was going to wait backstage for him, but I had to go to the little girl's room. I'd been traveling and all, had no time," she said, wrapping her fingers around the mug. "So, I'm in the cubicle fussing to get my jeans zipped, and these two girls are talking by the mirror, just on the other side of my door. And I do mean girls. I saw them before I went in, doing their lipstick and all. Fluffing their peroxide blonde hair. So, I hear one say to the other, 'You go with Dan tonight. I've got Derks like last night.' Derks! My Derks!"

"Uh oh," Olivia said.

Rachel didn't say anything, her eyes said it all.

"Yeah, right?" LuAnn said, looking at Olivia for support. "I'm in the cubicle, steaming. I was going to say something to the hussy, but they left before I could get my zipper to cooperate. After I primped a bit, I marched out of that little girl's room straight to the talent's dressing room. I was ready for bear!"

"Oh, LuAnn, I'm so sorry," Rachel said. "But what you heard could have been all on her, not Derks. He could have been innocent."

"Innocent? Is a child innocent when caught with his hand in the cookie jar?" LuAnn glared at Rachel. "Innocent? Far cry, you'll see. When I marched in there, everyone was having a party, getting ready to go somewhere to celebrate their success. Girls were everywhere, too. Not that it's unusual for groupies to hang out, but I don't know that some of those band members' wives would have appreciated what I saw their husbands doing. I didn't like what I saw Derks doing, that's for sure."

Neither Rachel nor Olivia commented. They quietly allowed LuAnn to rant while they sipped their iced teas.

"Derks had his arm around the one I heard talking in the little girl's room, giving her a kiss every once in a while. He was smiling. She was smiling. Everyone was smiling, except me. Then Dan, one of the bandmates, noticed me standing in the doorway," LuAnn said, frantically tapping the mug with her nails. "He looked over at Derks and nodded in my direction. When Derks turned to look over my way, his jaw dropped to his knees."

Olivia lowered her head. "Oh, my." Rachel kept watching LuAnn talk.

"Derks immediately dropped his arm from around the girl and came over to me. He was all, honey this and honey that. So sweet, like he always is. But I wasn't having it. No, sir." She took several swallows of her draft before she set her mug down. Her blue eyes were popping sparks. No one had ever seen her this way before, so angry and hurt.

"What did you do?" Rachel asked.

"I turned away from him with a swing of my arm, so he let loose of me. And I came home." LuAnn quieted down with a scowl on her face.

"You didn't say anything to him?" Olivia asked.

"Well, of course I did. Loudly. After I broke his hold on me. The others left us to fight it out. I was so hurt… just crushed. I went into the ugly cry. I mean, ugly, honey. Mascara running down my face. The green meanies ugly. It wasn't pretty."

"What did he say?" Rachel asked, toying with her glass.

"He gave me every excuse I had already heard before when a guy is caught misbehaving. He wasn't even the least bit original. 'She just came on me; she was aggressive; it was all her doing.' To which I said, 'So, what was your arm doing around her? Why were you kissing her?'"

"And he said?" Olivia asked, hanging on every word.

"He just looked at me, probably thinking I hadn't seen that part. Then I reminded him she had been with him the first night of the gig. I told him I overheard her talking in the little girl's room. Well, he didn't know what to say then. And he didn't deny being with her the night before. How could he? I heard what she said." LuAnn stopped talking. She sipped her draft and stared into space, slumped back in the chair.

Olivia and Rachel tried to talk to her, calm her down, but she remained silent, staring. Finally, LuAnn spoke.

"He broke my heart. Crushed it like a beer can," she said. "I had such high hopes for us. We were perfect together. And then he went on the road. Didn't I tell you this would happen?" LuAnn looked directly at Rachel, pointing her finger.

"Yes, you did."

"And it happened. I knew it before he even started packing," she said, throwing her hand into the air. "Bingo, he's gone, just like that."

Tears started chasing each other down her cheeks as she stared ahead. Rachel stood so she could place her arms around her friend. Olivia did the same. Both women comforted LuAnn until she stopped crying. Olivia pulled a tissue from her pocket and handed it to LuAnn. She wiped her eyes dry. Rachel sat back into her chair. Olivia stayed by LuAnn's side.

"What are you going to do?" Rachel asked.

LuAnn looked at her, sadness clearly decorating her eyes. "Continue with the gig I just got. Live here. Have friends like you two. Never speak to Derks again. That's over, for sure."

Olivia nodded. "I'm so glad I'm single."

THIRTY-FIVE

A FEW DAYS LATER, Rachel was lounging by the pool with Ruby and her fella. He looked pretty good in a bathing suit for a man of eighty-nine. His body appeared firm and he still had a shock of totally white hair growing on his head. Ruby sat with her sunhat on her head, watching Bob swimming in the pool. Rachel thought she looked like she had put on a few pounds since her ex-husband showed up. And she needed every one of them.

"I like your suit," Ruby said.

"Thanks. I got it at Dillard's. On sale, too." Rachel was stretched out on her chaise, sporting a black suit with wide white stripes swirling around her curves like a slinky.

"Where's your husband?"

"Getting educated about the Internet. Angie is showing him how she'll market the B and B."

"Very nice. I'm so glad she found her niche."

"Me, too." Rachel rolled over to face the woman. "And how are things going with you and Bob?"

Ruby rolled her face to the side so she could look at

Rachel. "You won't believe this, but we are talking marriage. At our age."

"Hey, Penelope and Alfred got married. What an odd couple. But they seem happy," she said, pointing across the pool.

Ruby turned her head to see Penelope and Alfred leaving the building and walking toward the garden. They were hand in hand, and both were beaming. "I'll be."

"They walk in the garden every day. It's romantic, don't you think?"

"Yes, I suppose it is. Good for them," Ruby said, turning her head back toward Rachel. "Maybe we will...hmm, someday..."

Rachel rolled onto her back, smiling. "What's the hold up?"

"I don't know. Our age? Certainly not money. We're both set for life." Ruby waved her hand in the air. "I don't know. Too many marriages?"

"Aw, what's one more, Ruby? It's sort of like cats, once you adopt one, what's another? How many marriages would that be?"

"None of your business. Let's just say, I could compete with Elizabeth Taylor."

Rachel laughed out loud.

"So, how did the class go?" Rachel asked in between bites of the meatloaf she had prepared. "Did your father learn anything new?"

Angie snickered, glancing over at her father. "Sort of."

"I learned to let her handle what she knows best," Joe said, pointing his fork at Angie. "All too complicated for my brain."

"Truth is, he could learn about websites, Facebook, and

other things, he just doesn't want to," Angie said with a smirk and a glint in her eye. "But that's okay. That's my job."

"How far did you get setting up?" Rachel asked.

"Well, I'm pleased to say, we now have a website and a Facebook account for the rentals," Angie said, helping herself to more green beans. "We are officially open for business."

"Really? Already?" Rachel put her fork onto her plate.

"Yup. Of course, I have to post things, market to real estate agents, travel firms, and so forth. It takes time to become recognized, so don't go thinking we'll have rentals for the weekend." Angie cautioned her mother's high hopes, knowing she didn't fully understand the process.

"I'm just happy you're doing all this for us," Rachel said. "And I'm proud of my smart little girl."

Angie looked over at her mother. Being called a little girl was almost laughable. Rachel was short in stature, while Angie stood at least eight inches above her mother. She hadn't been little for many years. However, "Thanks, Mom," was her response.

"What time are the Brighams coming over?" Joe asked.

"Eight o'clock." It had been Rachel's suggestion that they owed John and Josh an apology. They had accused Josh of the obvious, except he had been shown to be innocent. Josh had not, despite all indications, beat up James. While both men had threatened Rachel and Angie with bodily harm, Josh had not taken action against James, even though all the evidence seemed to point in that direction. No wonder John was so adamant that Angie retract her statement. His son really was innocent.

"Do I have to be here?" Angie asked.

"Of course. You're the one who originally came to the conclusion that Josh had sought revenge on the man. You have to be here." Rachel gave her daughter a stern look.

"Okay, if you say so," Angie said. "But it will be awkward."

"It will be awkward for all of us," Joe said. "So, we have to admit our guilt and apologize. Take our lumps, so to speak. That's what we do when we're wrong."

"Your father is right." Rachel put her napkin down and stood.

"Okay."

Everyone was ready ahead of time for their guests to arrive. Rachel made coffee and had bakery cookies available as a treat. When they heard the doorbell chime, each took a deep breath.

"Hello, come in," Rachel said, greeting the guests with a smile to cover her nerves.

John walked in stern-faced, while Josh attempted a smile.

"Come on into the living room," Joe said, leading the way for the two men.

Everyone took a seat while Rachel brought out a tray with the coffee decanter, mugs, sweeteners, cream, and cookies. Angie was already seated in a singular chair to avoid sitting near any one of the Brighams. John and Rachel sat next to each other on the couch while Josh and Joe were seated in the loveseat.

"Coffee, John?" Rachel asked, holding a mug in her hand while reaching for the decanter.

"Yes, thanks," he answered. He accepted the mug she gave him and waved off any sugar or cream.

"Josh?" Rachel looked across at the young man.

"Yes, thank you." Josh stood to receive the mug from Rachel. "Just black, thanks."

Joe shook his head no to the coffee but took the plate of cookies around to everyone.

"Angie?" she said to her daughter.

"No coffee for me, Mom." Angie looked up at her father standing in front of her and selected a cookie from the plate.

"I presume the police notified you that you are no longer a suspect regarding the murder of James Mason?" Rachel asked, sitting back into the comfort of the couch.

"Yes, they called me," Josh said. "There wasn't much of an explanation given, and frankly, I didn't care. I just wanted off the hook."

"We told the police you weren't the one," Rachel said, folding her hands in her lap and looking over at Josh. "It wasn't because of your threats of bodily harm to Angie and myself, either."

"Then why?" John asked, giving Rachel a suspicious look.

Angie joined the conversation. "I was at the beach a few days ago when I was recognized by a biker. I waited on him at the diner some months back during bike week. He started talking to me and my friend and mentioned James, although not by name."

"I don't understand," Josh said.

"Let her explain," Joe said.

"During the conversation, he talked about when James tried to pick me up and take me home that night after work. He and another biker saw what was happening and came to my rescue and walked me safely home." Angie was visibly nervous as she spoke, her hands moving and gripping each other. "He indicated to me that he had taken care of my situation; even gave me a wink."

Silence filled the room until John spoke. "You mean, the biker beat up this James fella?"

"Yes, exactly. I called the police right then so they could apprehend him in the area before he took off and became impossible to find among the other bikers."

Josh looked at Angie with a surprised expression. "Thank you."

"You're welcome. You didn't do it, as it turned out, so I was obligated to tell the police." Angie gave a slight smile to the young man. "I am truly sorry for all this mess. But you gave every indication to me that you had hurt the man. What was I to think? Well, apparently, I didn't think. I am sorry, Josh."

"It's okay. Not the first time I've been falsely accused," he said, giving her a smile.

"Maybe now we can stop the threats and be good neighbors?" Rachel asked. "That includes everyone in this complex. We can't have them being afraid of their neighbors."

"I think that can be arranged," John said, nodding before he took another sip of his coffee.

"Definitely," Josh said, also nodding, and then taking a bite of his cookie.

"You won't have any trouble from us," John said. "Long as my son is okay, I'm fine with everything. And you don't have to worry about any gambling going on here. Not that it ever did." Rachel and John shared a laugh.

After the Brighams left, Rachel and Joe went into their bedroom. Much to their surprise, Bennie and Precious were lying next to each other on the bed, sleeping.

"Will wonders never cease," Rachel said. "Finally, they are friends."

"I'll be…" Joe said as he glanced at the two felines while walking to the closet to retrieve his pajamas.

Both made haste in getting into bed. Once there, they prayed together. Among their prayers was gratitude for the unforeseen outcome with the Brighams. While they didn't wish to be friends with the two men, they certainly didn't want them as their enemies, either. The safety of their daughter was paramount in their hearts. Now that this ugly situation was behind them and the threats had ended, they could relax. Angie's future was looking bright, with her new vocation, not to mention the budding relationship with Brian. Rachel and Joe's world was bright and happy, thank God.

THIRTY-SIX

"LOOK HERE," Angie said, waving the newspaper in the air as she sat on the couch. "It says, 'Biker Arrested for Murder.'"

"Is that your murder case?" Rachel asked.

"Well, not exactly mine, but, yes, it's about James being attacked by a biker," she said, turning toward her mother sitting out on the balcony. "No bond given. They have strong DNA evidence, too. He's going to prison for sure."

"That's good news," Joe said from the balcony. "Why don't you come out and join us?"

"Okay." She moved outside to the empty chair. "I love these peaceful nights under the stars. After everything that's happened lately, this is so refreshing."

"How come you aren't with Brian tonight?" Rachel asked.

"He's working. This is my extra day off, so I can do my marketing." Angie smiled when she said marketing.

"He's a keeper, Angie," Joe said.

"Yes, he is. I got lucky. Oh, did I tell you we have renters coming?" she asked.

"When?" Rachel asked.

"On the weekend, for two nights," she said. "They're local

from Orlando, just wanting a weekend getaway near the beach. When they saw pictures of the B and B and the homey interior, they knew it was perfect for them."

"Good job, kiddo," Joe said. "I'll make sure it's spotless before they arrive."

"And after," she said.

"And after, yes," Joe said. He had cleanup duty after renters left. That was the deal.

"I have two potential couples coming the following weekend, but they haven't confirmed yet. As word of mouth gets out, we could attract lots of locals on weekends." Angie sighed her satisfaction.

"You're doing great, honey," Rachel said. "Now aren't you glad you came home?"

Angie thought for a few seconds before she spoke. "When I first arrived, I was wanting my independence, yet I was still clinging to you for support, not that I would have admitted such a thing. But it was time for me to take a leap of faith out of that comfy nest. I just didn't know it. Thanks to you two pushing at me to fly, I took the leap, spread my wings, and flew. Thanks for the push, guys."

"You're welcome," Joe said with a chuckle.

"But the other question is: are *you* glad I came home?" Angie asked.

Rachel laughed out loud. "I wasn't glad at all in the beginning. I thought this visit would be like all the rest. You'd have your hand out, wanting everything given to you. But thanks to your father's persistence in getting you to find a job, you didn't fall into the gimme mode. Not only that, but you also excelled. You found a job and have ambitions for the future. We are so proud of you, Angie." Rachel looked at her daughter, sprawled on the chair, beautiful in her casualness. "So, I'm delighted you came home. You have truly blossomed."

"We're both proud of you, honey. Just keep flying. You're on the right path." Joe settled into his chair with a deep sigh.

Angie looked up at the stars and the moon, sparkling down on her. In the distance she heard thunder. Rain probably wasn't even on the way, just a friendly rumble. So typical of Florida. She basked in the glow descending from the heavens, relishing the time she had spent with her parents. They were good people who had instilled good values in her, for which she was grateful. Yes, God is good.

Dear reader,

We hope you enjoyed reading *The Daughter* Please take a moment to leave a review, even if it's a short one. Your opinion is important to us.

Discover more books by Janie Owens at https://www.nextchapter.pub/authors/janie-owens

Want to know when one of our books is free or discounted? Join the newsletter at http://eepurl.com/bqqB3H

Best regards,

Janie Owens and the Next Chapter Team

Lightning Source UK Ltd.
Milton Keynes UK
UKHW020023160221
378843UK00012B/1338/J